"You're my boss."

"Not anymore," Conrad said with a satisfaction that started Sephy's heart thumping.

There was suddenly no doubt in Sephy's mind. *He was propositioning her.* "What…what are you saying exactly?" she asked at last.

"I want you, Sephy. I want you very badly. Is that clear enough? I would like to start seeing you—out of work. You've got under my skin in a way I can't explain."

"You are talking about a cheap affair, aren't you?" she said quietly.

"No, I am not."

HELEN BROOKS lives in Northamptonshire, England, and is married with three children. As she is a committed Christian, busy housewife and mother, her spare time is at a premium, but her hobbies include reading, swimming, gardening and walking her two energetic, inquisitive and very endearing young dogs. Her long-cherished aspiration to write became a reality when she put pen to paper on reaching the age of forty, and sent the result off to Harlequin.

Don't miss any of our special offers. Write to us at the following address for information on our newest releases.

Harlequin Reader Service
U.S.: 3010 Walden Ave., P.O. Box 1325, Buffalo, NY 14269
Canadian: P.O. Box 609, Fort Erie, Ont. L2A 5X3

Helen Brooks

THE MISTRESS CONTRACT

TORONTO • NEW YORK • LONDON
AMSTERDAM • PARIS • SYDNEY • HAMBURG
STOCKHOLM • ATHENS • TOKYO • MILAN • MADRID
PRAGUE • WARSAW • BUDAPEST • AUCKLAND

ISBN 0-373-12153-9

THE MISTRESS CONTRACT

First North American Publication 2001.

CHAPTER ONE

'ME?' SEPHY stared at Mrs Williams—the company secretary's assistant—in horror, her velvet-brown eyes opening wide as she said again, 'Me? Stand in for Mr Quentin's secretary? I don't think I could, Pat. I mean—'

'Of course you could,' Pat Williams interrupted briskly, her sharp voice, which matched her sharp face and thin, angular body, signalling that the matter was not open for discussion. 'You're as bright as a button, Seraphina, even if you do insist on hiding your light under a bushel most of the time, and after six years at Quentin Dynamics you know as much as me about the firm and its operating procedures. More, probably, after working for Mr Harper in Customer Support and Service for four years.'

Sephy smiled weakly. The Customer Support and Services department was, by its very nature, a fast-moving and hectic environment within Quentin Dynamics, and in her position as assistant to Mr Harper—who was small and plump and genial, but the sort of boss who arrived late, left early and had three-hour lunch breaks most days—she was used to dealing with the hundred and one panics that erupted daily on her own initiative. But Mr Harper and Customer Service was one thing; Conrad Quentin, the millionaire entrepreneur and tycoon founder of the firm, was quite another!

Sephy took a deep breath and said firmly, 'I really don't think it's a good idea, Pat. I'm sorry, but I'm sure there must be someone else more suitable? What about Jenny Brown, Mr Eddleston's secretary? Or Suzy Dodds? Or... or you?'

The other woman waved a dismissive bony hand. 'Those two girls would last ten minutes with Mr Quentin and you know it, and with the end of year accounts to pull together I can't desert Mr Meadows. No, you're ideal. You know the ins and outs of the business, you've got a level head on your shoulders, and you're used to dealing with awkward customers every day of the week so Mr Quentin won't throw you. We can get a good temp to fill in for you until Mr Quentin's secretary is back—'

'Can't Mr Quentin have the good temp?' Sephy interjected desperately.

'He'd eat her alive!' Pat's beady black eyes held Sephy's golden-brown ones. 'You know how impatient he is. He hasn't got time for someone who doesn't know the ropes, besides which he expects his secretary to practically live here, and most girls have got—' She stopped abruptly, suddenly aware she was being tactless as Sephy's small heart-shaped face flushed hotly.

'Most girls have got boyfriends or husbands or whatever,' Sephy finished flatly.

Sephy had never hidden the fact that she rarely dated and that her social diary wasn't exactly the most riveting reading, but it wasn't particularly warming to think that Pat Williams—along with everyone else, most probably— thought she had nothing better to do than work twenty-four hours a day.

'Well, yes,' Pat murmured uncomfortably.

'What about Marilyn?'

'Tried her first, lasted an hour.'

'Philippa?'

'Howled her eyes out in the ladies' cloakroom all lunchtime and has gone home with a migraine,' Pat said triumphantly. 'She's not used to men snapping and snarling at her like Mr Quentin did.'

Sephy thought of the beautiful ash-blonde who was the

marketing manager's secretary, and who had different men in flash, expensive sports cars waiting outside the building for her every night of the week and nodded. 'No, I can imagine,' she agreed drily. 'And you think I am, is that it?'

'Seraphina, *please*. Try it for this afternoon at least.' In spite of the 'please' it was more of an order than a request, and Sephy stared at the other woman exasperatedly.

Pat Williams was the only person she knew—apart from her mother—who insisted on giving her her full Christian name when she knew full well Sephy loathed it, but it went with the brusque, army-style manner of the company secretary's assistant, and the utilitarian haircut and severely practical clothes.

For her first two years at Quentin Dynamics, Sephy— along with the other secretaries and personnel of the hugely successful software firm that majored in specialist packages for different types of companies—had thoroughly disliked Pat Williams, but there had come a day when she and the other woman had been working late and she had found Pat in the ladies' cloakroom in tears.

All Pat's defences had been down, and when Sephy had discovered her history—an upbringing in a children's home where she'd met the husband she adored, only for him to develop multiple sclerosis just after they married, which now confined him to a wheelchair and made Pat the bread-winner—her friendship with the older woman had begun.

And it was that which made Sephy sigh loudly, narrow her eyes and nod her dark head resignedly. 'One afternoon,' she agreed quietly. 'But I can't see me lasting any better than the others, Pat. It's a well-known fact Madge Watkins is so devoted to him she puts up with anything, and she's been his secretary for decades! How can anyone step into her shoes?'

'She's been his secretary for thirteen years,' Pat corrected cheerfully, allowing herself a smile now Sephy had agreed to help her out of what had become a very tight spot. 'And I'm not asking you to step into her shoes; they wouldn't fit you.'

They both thought of the elderly spinster, who looked like a tiny shrivelled up prune but was excellent at her job, and absolutely ruthless when it came to ensuring that her esteemed boss's life ran like clockwork with lesser mortals kept very firmly in their place. 'How long is she expected to be in hospital?' Sephy asked flatly.

'Not sure.' Pat eyed her carefully. 'She was rushed in in the middle of the night with stomach pains and they're talking about doing an exploratory op today or tomorrow.'

Wonderful. Sephy sighed long and loudly and left it to Pat to inform Ted Harper that his secretary and right-hand man—or woman, in this case—had been commandeered for the foreseeable future. He wouldn't like it—he might have to start working for that sizeable salary he picked up each month—but he wouldn't argue. Everyone fell down and worshipped at the feet of the illustrious head of Quentin Dynamics, and it wouldn't occur to any of Conrad Quentin's staff to deny him anything, Sephy thought wryly.

Not that she had had anything to do with him, to be fair, but it was common knowledge that thirteen years ago, at the age of twenty-five, Conrad Quentin had had a meteoric rise in the business world, and his power and wealth were legendary. As was his taste for beautiful women. He was the original love 'em and leave 'em type, but, judging by the number of times his picture appeared in the paper with a different glittering female hanging adoringly on his arm at some spectacular function or other, one had to assume his attraction outshone his reputation.

Or perhaps the sort of women Conrad Quentin chose thought they were beautiful and desirable enough to tame the wolf? Sephy's clear brow wrinkled. Maybe they even relished the challenge? Whatever, in spite of his well-publicised affairs over the years, with some of the precious darlings of the jet-set, no one had managed to snare him yet.

Oh, what was she doing wasting time thinking about Mr Quentin's love-life? Sephy shook herself irritably and then quickly fixed her face in a purposely blank expression as Pat sailed out of Ted Harper's office and said cheerfully, 'Right, that's settled, then. I've told him I'll get a temp here for tomorrow morning and he can manage for one afternoon. Are you ready?'

For Conrad Quentin? *Absolutely not.* 'Yes, I'm ready,' Sephy said, with what she considered admirable calm in the circumstances, resisting the temptation to nip to the ladies' cloakroom. All the titivating in the world wouldn't make any difference to the medium height, gentle-eyed, dark-haired girl who would stare back at her from the long rectangular mirror above the three basins.

She wasn't plain, she knew that, but she was...nondescript, she admitted silently as she followed Pat out of the office and along the corridor towards the lift for the exalted top floor. Her honey-brown eyes, shoulder-length thick brown hair and small neat nose were all pleasant, but unremarkable, and to cap it all she had an abundance of freckles scattered across her smooth, creamy skin that made her look heaps younger than her twenty-six years.

'Here we are, then.' They had emerged from the lift and Pat was being deliberately hearty as she led Sephy past her own office and that of the company secretary and financial director. Conrad Quentin's vast suite took up all the rest of the top floor, and to say the opulence was intimidating was putting it mildly. 'Your home from home for the next little while.'

'I said an afternoon, Pat,' Sephy hissed quietly as the other woman opened the door in front of them. Sephy had visited the top floor a few times—rapid calls which had lasted as long as the delivery of files or whatever had necessitated—and she found the lavish surroundings somewhat surreal. 'He's bound to treat me the same as the rest.'

'And how, exactly, did I treat the rest, Miss…?'

Sephy heard Pat's sudden intake of breath, but all her senses were focused on the tall, dark man who had obviously been about to leave the room when they had opened the door. She had spoken to Conrad Quentin a few times in the six years she had been working at the firm—brief, polite words at the obligatory Christmas party and on the rare occasions their paths had crossed in the lift—but she had always been overcome with nerves at the prospect of saying the wrong thing and had escaped at the earliest opportunity. But now she certainly *had* said the wrong thing, and there was no retreat possible.

She stared desperately into the hard, chiselled face; the piercing blue of his eyes threw his tanned skin into even more prominence, picking up the ebony sheen in his jet-black hair, and she saw his straight black eyebrows were lifted in mockingly cruel enquiry.

And it did something to her, causing anger to slice through her body and tighten her stomach, and before she knew she had spoken she said, her voice tight and very controlled, 'You know that better than me, Mr Quentin,' and held his glance.

Pat looked as if she was going to faint at the side of her, and for the first time ever Sephy heard the company secretary's cool dragon of a secretary babbling as she said, 'This is Seraphina, Mr Quentin, from Customer Services. She's been with us six years and I thought she would be suitable for temporarily standing in for Miss Watkins. Of course, if you think—'

The man in front of them raised an authoritative hand

and immediately Pat's voice was cut off. 'You think I treat my staff unfairly, Seraphina?' he asked silkily.

All sorts of things were racing through Sephy's frantic mind. She couldn't believe she had spoken to Conrad Quentin like that, and her heart was pounding like a drum even as tiny pinpricks of sheer, unmitigated panic hit every nerve and sinew. This could be the end of her extremely well-paid and interesting job. And the end of her job could threaten the new flat she had just moved into, the flat it had taken so long to find. And if she left with a black mark over her, if he refused to allow Mr Harper to give her a good reference, how soon could she get other work?

Conrad Quentin was the ultimate in ruthlessness—everyone, *everyone* knew that—and people didn't talk back to him! People didn't even *breathe* without his say-so. She must have had a brainstorm; it was the only explanation. Maybe if she grovelled low enough he'd overlook the matter?

And then something in the icy sapphire gaze told her he knew exactly what she was thinking and that he was fully expecting her to abase herself.

In the split second it took for the decision to be made Sephy heard herself saying, 'If everything I have heard is true it would appear so, Mr Quentin, but not having worked for you personally I can't be positive, of course.' And she raised her small chin a notch higher as she waited for the storm to break over her head.

As he stared at her she was aware that the hard, masculine face—which just missed being handsome and instead held a magnetic attractiveness that was a thousand times more compelling than any pretty-boy good looks—was betraying nothing of what he was feeling. It was unnerving. Very unnerving. And she would dare bet her life he was fully aware of just that very thing.

'Then we had better rectify that small point so that you

can make a judgement based on fact rather than hearsay,' he said smoothly, inclining his head towards Pat as he added, 'Thank you, Pat. I'm sure Seraphina is capable of managing on her own.' The tone was not complimentary.

'Yes, of course. I was just going to show her where everything is…the filing cabinets and so on… But, yes, of course…' Pat had backed out of the doorway as she had spoken, her one glance at Sephy saying quite clearly, You rather than me, kid, but you asked for it! before she shut the door behind her, leaving Sephy standing in front of the brilliant and eminent head of Quentin Dynamics.

He was very tall. The observation came from nowhere and it didn't help Sephy's confidence. And big—muscle-type big—with a leanness that suggested regular workouts and a passion for fitness.

'So you have worked for Quentin Dynamics for six years?'

His voice was deep, with an edge of huskiness that took it out of the ordinary and into the unforgettable. Sephy took several steadying breaths until she was sure her voice was under control, and then she said quietly, 'Yes, that's right. That's one of the reasons Pat thought you would prefer me to a temp.'

'I don't use temps.'

The laser-blue eyes hadn't left hers for a moment, and Sephy was finding it incredibly difficult not to give in to the temptation to drop her gaze. 'Oh…' She didn't know what else to say.

'My secretary always aligns her holidays with mine and she is rarely ill,' he continued coolly. 'It doesn't fit in with my schedule.'

The sweeping pretension brought her thickly lashed eyes widening, before she saw the mocking glint in his own and said weakly, 'You're joking.'

'Many a true word is spoken in jest, Seraphina.'

They were standing in the outer office, part of which was kitted out as a small reception area. Deep easy seats were clustered around a couple of wood tables laden with glossy magazines, to the side of which were lush potted palms and a water chiller. Now he turned and walked past the sitting area to where his secretary's huge desk and chair stood, just in front of the interconnecting door to his office.

There was a row of superior filing cabinets in an alcove at the back of the desk, and he flicked one tanned wrist as he passed, saying, 'Acquaint yourself with those immediately. The more confidential files are kept in my office, along with data and documents relating to my other interests outside Quentin Dynamics. There are two sets of keys.' He turned in the doorway to his rooms and again the blue gaze raked her face with its cold perusal. 'I have one set and Miss Watkins has the other. Hopefully it will not be necessary to retrieve those from her; I am anticipating she will soon be back at her desk again.'

Not as much as she was, Sephy thought with a faint touch of hysteria. Suddenly Mr Harper and her battered little desk in Customer Services took on the poignancy of an oasis in the desert and she felt positively homesick.

Mr Harper might be work-shy and somewhat somnolent most of the time, and his personal hygiene was distinctly iffy on occasion, but he was rotund and genial and utterly devoted to his wife and children, and their ever-expanding family of grandchildren.

Conrad Quentin, on the other hand, was like a brilliant black star that kept all the lesser planets orbiting it in a perpetual state of fermenting unrest. It wasn't just the knowledge that he was a multimillionaire with a well-deserved reputation for ruthless arrogance, who demanded one hundred per cent commitment from his employees—it was *him*, the man himself. The harsh, flagrantly male features and muscular physique had a sensualness about them that was overwhelming.

His virile maleness was emphasised rather than concealed by the wildly expensive clothes he wore, and the unmistakable aura of wealth and power was so real she could taste it. He was everything she disliked in a man.

Still, she didn't have to like him, she reminded herself sharply, as she became aware he was waiting for her reply. She managed a careful, impersonal smile and said politely, 'I'm sure she will, Mr Quentin.' No, she didn't have to like him, and with any luck the resilient Madge, who was about four-foot-ten and looked as if a breath of wind would blow her away but must have the toughness of a pair of old boots to have lasted this long with her high-powered, vigorous boss, would be back at her desk within the week.

Not that she had much chance of lasting a week—half a day would be doing pretty good, Sephy thought ruefully.

He nodded abruptly, closing the interconnecting door as he said, 'Twenty minutes, Seraphina, and then I'd like you in here with the Breedon file, the Einhorn file and notebook and pencil.'

Pat, Pat, Pat... As the door closed Sephy leant limply against Madge's desk for a moment. How could you blackmail me with friendship into this position?

And then she straightened sharply as the door opened again and he poked his head round to say, 'Why haven't I seen you before if you've worked here for six years?' as though she had purposely been hiding in a cupboard all that time.

It was on the tip of her tongue to answer tartly, Because I'm not a model-type *femme fatale* with long blonde hair and the sort of figure that drives men wild—the type of woman Conrad Quentin usually went for if the newspaper pictures were to be believed—but a very ordinary, brown-haired, brown-eyed, slightly plump little nobody. But she felt that would be pushing her luck too far. Instead she gritted her teeth, forced a smile, and said quietly, 'You have seen me, Mr Quentin. We have spoken on at least two or three occasions.'

'Have we?' He frowned darkly. 'I don't remember.'

He clearly considered it her fault, and she was prompted to retort, with an asperity it was difficult to temper, 'There's no reason why you should, is there? You're a very busy man, after all.' He was often abroad on business, and Quentin Dynamics was only one of his many enterprises, all of which seemed to have the Midas touch, and it was to this Sephy referred as she added quickly, 'You can't know everyone who works for you, and the way you've expanded over the years...'

'I trust that is a reference to my business acumen and not my waistline?' And he smiled. Just a quick flash of white teeth as he closed the door again, but it was enough to leave her standing in stunned silence for some long moments. The difference it had made to his hard cold face, the way his piercing blue eyes had crinkled and mellowed and his uncompromising jawline softened, had been...well, devastating, she admitted unsteadily. And it bothered her more than anything else that had happened that day.

But she couldn't think of it now. She seized on the thought like a lifeline and took a deep, shuddering breath as she glanced towards the filing cabinets. She was here to stand in for the formidable Madge and she had to make some sort of reasonable stab at it. She had been used to looking after Mr Harper for four years and virtually carrying that office at times; she could do this. *She could.*

Twenty minutes later to the dot she knocked at the interconnecting door, the files and her notebook and pencil tucked under one arm.

She wished she had worn something newer and smarter than the plain white blouse and straight black skirt she had pulled on that morning, but it was too late now. They were serviceable enough, but distinctly utilitarian, and because she had overslept she hadn't bothered to put her hair up, as normal, or apply any eye make-up.

Oh, stop fussing! The admonition came just as she heard the deep 'Come in' from inside the room. Conrad Quentin wouldn't be looking at *her*, Sephy Vincent. He wanted an efficient working machine, and as long as she met that criterion all would be well.

She opened the door and walked briskly into the vast expanse in front of her. The far wall of the room, in front of which Conrad Quentin had his enormous desk and chair, was all glass. Before she reached the chair he gestured at, Sephy was conscious of a breathtaking view of half of London coupled with a spacious luxury that made Mr Harper's little office seem like a broom cupboard.

'Sit down, Seraphina.'

That was the fourth or fifth time; she'd have to say something. 'It's Sephy, actually,' she said steadily as she sat in the plushly upholstered armless chair in front of the walnut desk, crossing her legs and then forcing herself to look at him. 'I never use my full name.'

'Why not?' He had been sitting bent over piles of papers he'd been scrutinising, but now he raised his head and sat back in the enormous leather chair, clasping his hands behind his head as he surveyed her through narrowed blue eyes. 'What's wrong with it?'

The pose had brought powerful chest muscles into play beneath the thin grey silk of the shirt he was wearing, and at some time in the last twenty minutes he had loosened his tie and undone the top buttons of his shirt, exposing the shadow of dark body hair at the base of his throat.

Sephy cleared her dry throat. 'It doesn't suit me. Even my mother had to agree she'd made a mistake, but I was born on the twelfth of March, and on the calendar of saints Seraphina is the only woman for that day.'

He said nothing, merely shifted position slightly in the black chair, and now she was horrified to find herself beginning to waffle as she said, 'Mind, it could have been worse. There's a Gertrude and a Euphemia in the next few days, so perhaps I ought to be thankful for small mercies. But Seraphina suggests an ethereal, will-o'-the-wisp type creature, and I'm certainly not that.'

He leant forward again, the glittering sapphire gaze moving over her creamy skin, soft mouth and wide honey-brown eyes, and he stared at her a moment before he said, his tone expressionless, 'I think Seraphina suits you and I certainly don't intend to call you by such a ridiculous abbreviation as Sephy. It's the sort of name one would bestow on a pet poodle. Have you a second Christian name?'

'No.' It was something of a snap.

'Pity,' he said laconically.

She didn't believe this. How dared he ride roughshod over her wishes? she asked herself silently. She was searching her mind for an adequately curt response when he switched to sharp business mode, his eyes turning to the papers spread out over his desk as he said, his tone keen and focused, 'How familiar are you with the Einhorn project?'

As luck would have it she had been dealing with the problems associated with this particular package over the last weeks, and she had just spent ten of the last twenty minutes delving into the file to see if there were any confidential complications Customer Services hadn't been privy to. 'Quite familiar,' she answered smartly.

'Really?' He raised his dark head and the hard sapphire gaze homed in. 'Tell me what you know.'

She considered for a moment or two, trying to pull her thoughts into concise order, and then spoke quietly and fluently as she outlined what had been a disastrous endeavour from the start, due to a series of mistakes which Sephy felt could be laid fair and square at Quentin Dynamics' door.

He looked down at his desk as she began talking, a frown creasing his brow as he listened intently without glancing at her once. As she finished speaking the frown became a quizzical ruffle, and he raised his head and said, 'Brains *and* beauty! Well, well, well. Have I found myself a treasure, here?' And then, before she could respond in any way, 'So, you think we should take the full hit on this? Reimburse for engineering call-out charges as well as a free upgrade for the software?'

It probably wasn't very clever to tell him his company had made a sow's ear out of what should have been a silk purse within the first half an hour of working with him, but Sephy took a deep breath and said firmly, 'Yes, I do.'

'And Mr Ransome's report, that recommends we merely reduce the cost for the new software?'

Mr Ransome was trying to cover his own shortcomings with regard to the whole sorry mess, but Sephy didn't feel she could be that blunt.

She didn't answer immediately, and the blue eyes narrowed before she said quietly, 'He's wrong, in my opinion, and although the firm might save a good deal of money in the short term, I don't think it will do Quentin Dynamics' reputation any good in the long term.'

He gave her a long hard look. 'Right. And you think that is important?'

'Very.' Now it was her turn to hold his eyes. 'Don't you?'

He folded his arms over his chest, settling back in his seat again as he surveyed her thoughtfully. The white sunlight streaming in through the plate glass at the back of him was picking up what was almost a blue sheen in his jet-black hair, and Sephy was aware of the unusual thickness of the black lashes shading the vivid blue eyes as she looked back at him.

He had something. The thought popped into her consciousness with a nervous quiver. Male magnetism; a dark fascination; good old-fashioned sex appeal—call it what you will, it was there and it was powerful. Oh, boy, was it powerful!

'Yes, I do,' he said quietly. He stared at her a moment more and then snapped forward, speaking swiftly and softly as he outlined various procedures he wanted put into place. 'Internal memos to Customer Services, Marketing and Research,' he added shortly. 'You can see to those, I presume? And a letter to Einhorn stating what we have decided. And I want a complete breakdown from Accounts of all costs.'

'You want me to write the memos and the letter?' Sephy asked quickly as he paused for breath.

'Certainly.' The piercing gaze flashed upwards from the papers on the desk. 'That's not a problem, is it? I need my secretary to work on her own initiative most of the time, once I've made any overall decisions. I can't be bothered with trivialities.'

Sephy nodded somewhat dazedly. She could see Madge earnt every penny of her salary.

He continued to fire instructions and brief guidelines on a whole host of matters for some few minutes more, and by the time Sephy rose to walk back to Madge's desk she felt as though she had been run over by a steamroller.

She had enough work to last her two or three days and she had only been in there a matter of minutes, she told herself weakly as she plopped down on her chair. He was amazing. Intelligent—acutely intelligent—and with a razor-sharp grasp of what was at the heart of any matter that cut straight through incidentals and exposed the kernel in the nut.

And he scared her to death.

She worked solidly for the rest of the afternoon, her fingers flying over the keys of the word processor as the pile of papers for signature grew. Apart from telephone calls and a brief stop for coffee—delivered on a silver tray from the small canteen at the basement of the building by one of the staff and drunk at her desk—she didn't raise her head from the screen, and it came as something of a shock when she glanced at her wristwatch just after half past five.

She quickly gathered up all the correspondence awaiting signature and knocked at the interconnecting door, hearing the deep 'Come in' as butterflies began to flutter in her stomach.

He glanced up from his hand-held dictating machine as she entered, his expression preoccupied. He had been running his hand through his hair, if the ruffled black crop was anything to go by, and the tie had gone altogether now, along with a couple more buttons being undone, which exposed a V of tanned flesh and dark curling body hair.

The butterflies joined together in an explosive tarantella, and Sephy forced herself to concentrate very hard on a point just over his left shoulder as she smiled brightly and walked across to his desk. 'Correspondence for signature,' she squeaked, clearing her throat before adding, 'The post goes at six, so if you could look at them now, please? I didn't realise what the time was.'

He glanced at the gold Rolex on his wrist. 'Hell!'

'What's the matter?' Sephy asked guardedly.

'I've a dinner engagement at seven,' he muttered abstractedly. 'Look, ring her, would you? Explain about Madge, and that things are out of kilter here, and say I'll be half an hour late. She won't like it—' he grimaced slightly '—but don't stand any nonsense.'

'Ring who?'

'What?' He clearly expected her to be a mind-reader, as no doubt the faithful Madge was. 'Oh, Caroline de Menthe; the number's in here.'

He threw the obligatory little black book which he'd fetched out of a drawer across the desk.

'Right.' She took a deep breath and let it out evenly. She had heard of Caroline de Menthe. Everyone in the *world* had heard of the statuesque French model, who had the body of a goddess and the face of an angel and who was the toast of London and every other capital city besides. And she was his date. Of course she was. She was the latest prize on the circuit so she'd be bound to be, wouldn't she? Sephy thought with a shrewishness that surprised her.

Once back at her desk she thumbed through the book, trying to ignore the reams of female names, and then, once she had found Caroline de Menthe, dialled the London number—there were several international numbers under the same name. She spoke politely into the receiver when she got through to the Savoy switchboard.

It was a moment or two before Reception connected her, and then a sultry, heavily accented voice said lazily, 'Caroline de Menthe.'

'Good afternoon, Miss de Menthe,' Sephy said quickly. 'Mr Quentin has asked me to call you to say he is sorry but he'll be half an hour late this evening. His secretary has been taken ill and he is running a little behind schedule. He will pick you up at about half past seven if that is all right?'

'And you are what? An office girl?' The seductive sultriness was gone; the other woman's tone was distinctly vinegary now.

'I am standing in for Mr Quentin's secretary,' Sephy stated quietly, forcing herself not to react to the overt rudeness.

There was a moment's silence, and then the model said curtly, 'Tell Mr Quentin I will be waiting for him,' and the phone went dead.

Charming. Sephy stared at the receiver in her hand for a moment before slowly replacing it. Caroline de Menthe might be beautiful and famous and have the world at her feet, but she didn't have the manners of an alley cat. She glanced at the interconnecting door as she wrinkled her small nose. And that was the sort of woman he liked? Still, it was absolutely nothing to do with her. She was just his temporary secretary—*very* temporary.

The telephone rang, cutting off further deliberations, and when she realised it was the hospital asking for Mr Quentin she put the call through to him immediately.

It was a minute or two before the call ended and he buzzed her at once. She opened the door to see him sitting back in his chair with a stunned look on his dark face. 'It's cancer,' he said slowly. 'The poor old girl's got cancer.'

'Oh, no. Oh, I'm so sorry,' Sephy said helplessly. He looked poleaxed and positively grey, and she was amazed how much he obviously cared.

'They think it's operable and that she'll be okay in the long run, but it'll be a long job,' he said flatly, after taking a hard pull of air. And then he made Sephy jump a mile as he drove his fist down on to the desk with enough force to make the papers rise an inch or two. 'Damn stupid woman,' he ground out through clenched teeth. 'Why didn't she *say* something? The consultant said she must have been in pain for some weeks.'

'She probably thought it was viral, something like that,' Sephy pointed out sensibly. 'No one likes to think the worst.'

'Spare me the benefit of inane female logic,' he bit back with cutting coldness.

She swallowed hard. Okay, so he was obviously upset

about Madge, and she would ignore his rudeness this time, but if he thought she was going to be a doormat he'd got another think coming! She wouldn't take that from anyone.

'Hell!' It was an angry bark. 'This is going to hit her hard. Her job is her life, it's what makes her tick, and she's been with me from the start. She'll hate the idea of being laid low, and she's got no friends, just a sister somewhere or other.'

Sephy remained silent. This was awful for Madge, and difficult for him, but once bitten, twice shy. She was saying nothing.

'So...' He rose from the desk and turned to the window so his back was towards her. 'She's covered by the company's private health plan, but make sure she's in the best room available; any additional costs will be covered by me personally. And send her some flowers and chocolates and a selection of magazines. Is there anything else you, as another woman, would think she'd like?' he asked, turning to face her with characteristic abruptness.

She stared at him. 'A visit?' she suggested pointedly.

His eyes narrowed into blue slits and he was grimly silent for a full ten seconds before he said expressionlessly, 'I don't like hospitals,' as though that was the end of the matter.

'If she's as lacking in friends as you said she'd still like a visit,' Sephy said stolidly. 'She must be feeling very vulnerable tonight, and probably a bit frightened.'

She saw his square jaw move as his teeth clenched hard and then he sighed irritably, a scowl crossing his harsh attractive face. 'She's probably exhausted right now,' he snapped tightly. 'It doesn't *have* to be tonight, does it?'

Sephy thought of the ravishing Caroline de Menthe waiting at the Savoy and smiled sweetly. 'That's up to you, of course, but a little bit of reassurance at a time like this goes a long way,' she said with saccharine gentleness.

She gathered up the pile of correspondence, now duly signed, as she spoke, and then felt awful about the covert bitchiness when he said, his tone distracted, 'That's excellent work by the way, Seraphina. I trust you've no objection to standing in for Madge for the next few weeks?'

She hesitated for a moment, his big, broad-shouldered body and rugged face swimming into focus as she raised her head from the papers in her hands, and then, as he raised enquiring black eyebrows she forced herself to smile coolly. 'Of course not,' she lied with careful composure. 'If you think I'm up to the job, that is.'

'I don't think there is any doubt about that,' he returned drily, the deep-blue eyes which resembled a cold summer sea watching her intently. 'No doubt at all.'

And this time he didn't smile.

CHAPTER TWO

QUENTIN DYNAMICS occupied a smart, four-storey building in Islington and Sephy's new flat was just a ten-minute walk away, which was wonderful after years of battling on the train from Twickenham.

The late September evening was mellow and balmy as she trod the crowded London pavements, and the chairs and tables outside most of the pubs and cafés were full as Londoners enjoyed an alfresco drink in the Indian summer the country was enjoying.

Everyone seemed relaxed and easy now the working day was finished, but Sephy was conscious that she felt somewhat stunned as she walked along in the warm, traffic-scented air, and more tired than she had felt in a long, long time.

Mind you, that wasn't surprising, she reassured herself silently in the next moment. She always worked hard—as Mr Harper's secretary she was used to working on her own initiative and dealing with one panic after another most days—but being around Conrad Quentin was something else again! The man wasn't human—he was a machine that consumed facts and figures with spectacular single-mindedness and with a swiftness that was frightening.

No wonder he had risen so dramatically fast to the top of his field, she thought ruefully as she neared the row of shops over which her flat—and ten others—were situated. Other men might have his astute business sense and brilliance, but they were lacking the almost monomaniacal drive of the head of Quentin Dynamics.

Was he like that in all areas of his life? A sudden picture

25

of Caroline de Menthe was there on the screen on her mind, along with the long list of women's names in the little black book he had tossed to her. It was an answer in itself and it made Sephy go hot inside.

He would be an incredible lover; of course he would! He had lush beauties absolutely *panting* after him, and inevitably they were reduced to purring pussycats by the magnetism that surrounded him like a dark aura, if all the society photographs and office gossip were anything to go by.

He was king of the small kingdom he had created, an invincible being who had only to click his fingers to see his minions falling over themselves to please him. And he knew it.

She didn't know why it bothered her so much but it did. Sephy was frowning as she delved in her shoulder bag for her keys to unlock the outside door, behind which were stairs leading to the front door of her flat, and the frown deepened as she heard Jerry's voice call her name.

Jerry was the young owner of the menswear shop, and nice enough, even good-looking in a floppy-haired kind of way, but although Sephy liked him she knew she could never think of him in a romantic sense. He was too...boyish.

Jerry, on the other hand, seemed determined to pursue her, even after she had told him—politely but firmly—that there was no chance of a date. It made her feel uncomfortable, even guilty, when he was so likeable and friendly, as though she was smacking down a big amiable puppy with dirty feet who wanted to play.

She raised her eyes, her hand still in her bag, and turned her head to see Jerry just behind her, the very epitome of public school Britain in his immaculate flannels and well-pressed shirt.

'Just wanted to remind you about Maisie's party tonight,' he said earnestly. 'You hadn't forgotten?'

She had. Maisie occupied the flat two doors along, above her own boutique, and her psychedelic hair—dyed several vivid colours and gelled to stick up in dangerous-looking spikes—and enthusiastic body-piercing hid a very intelligent and shrewd mind. And Maisie's parties were legendary. The trouble was—Sephy's eyes narrowed just the slightest as her mind raced—Maisie and all of Jerry's other friends knew how he felt about her and, ever since she had moved into the flat, some eight weeks ago, had been trying to pair them off.

She had just opened her mouth to give voice to the weakest excuse of all—a blinding headache, which had every likelihood of being perfectly true the way her head was thumping after the hectic day—when a deep cold voice cut through the balmy evening air like a knife through butter.

'It would have been quicker to walk here with this damn traffic.'

'Mr Quentin!' She had whirled right round to face the road at the sound of his voice and her heart seemed to stop, and then race on like a greyhound.

Conrad Quentin was sitting at the wheel of a silver Mercedes, the driver's window down and his arm resting on the ledge as he surveyed her lazily from narrowed blue eyes in the fading light. The big beautiful car, the dark, brooding quality of its inhabitant and the utter surprise of it all robbed Sephy of all coherent thought, and it was a few moments before the mocking sapphire gaze told her she was looking at him with her mouth open.

She shut her lips so suddenly her teeth jarred, and then made a superhuman effort to pull herself together as she muttered in a soft aside to Jerry, 'It's my boss from work,' before walking quickly across the pavement to the side of the waiting vehicle.

'One set of keys.' He spoke before she could say anything. 'I noticed them on the floor as I was leaving and thought they might be important?' he added quietly as he handed her the keyring.

She stared at the keys for a moment before raising her burning face to his cool perusal. Her flat keys, the keys to her mother's house and car, as well as those for Mr Harper's office and the filing cabinets. What must he be thinking? she asked herself hotly. It wasn't exactly reassuring to think one's temporary secretary was in the habit of mislaying such items. *Ex*-temporary secretary!

'I dropped my bag earlier.' It was a monotone, but all she could manage. 'They must have fallen out.'

'Undoubtedly.' It was very dry.

'Tha...thank you.' Oh, don't stutter! Whatever else, don't *stutter*, she told herself heatedly.

'My pleasure.' He eyed her sardonically.

'It was when the fax from Einhorn came through,' she said quickly. 'I knew you were waiting for it and I knocked my bag off the desk as I went to reach for it. I must have missed the keys...' Her voice trailed away weakly. It could have been *his* keys she'd dropped, the keys to his confidential papers and so on, if he had retrieved Madge's set. Which he hadn't yet. And when he did, he was hardly likely to give them to her now, was he? she belaboured herself miserably. He must think she was a featherbrain! And she'd never done anything like this with Mr Harper.

'No one is perfect, Seraphina.' And then he further surprised her when he added, the brilliant blue eyes holding hers, 'It's a relief, actually. I was beginning to think I'd have my work cut out to keep up with you.'

Her mouth was open again but she couldn't help it.

'So...' His dark husky voice was soft and low. 'Is that the boyfriend?' The blue eyes looked past her and they were mocking.

'What?' She was still recovering from being let off the hook.

'The guy who is glaring at me.' It was a slow, amused drawl. 'Is he your boyfriend?'

Belatedly she remembered Jerry, and as she turned her head, following the direction of Conrad Quentin's eyes, she saw Jerry was indeed glaring. 'No, no of course not,' she said distractedly. 'He's just a neighbour, a friend.'

The black eyebrows went a notch higher. 'Really?' It was cryptic.

'Yes, really,' she snapped back, before she remembered this was Conrad Quentin she was talking to. 'He...he owns the shop below my flat,' she said more circumspectly. 'That's all.' And then she added, as the vivid blue gaze became distinctly uncomfortable, 'Thank you so much for bringing the keys, and I'm sorry to have put you to so much trouble.'

'How sorry?' he asked smoothly.

'What?' It was becoming a habit, this 'what?', but then she might have known he wouldn't react like ninety-nine per cent of people would to her gracious little speech, she told herself silently.

'I said, how sorry?' he drawled lazily, the sapphire eyes as sharp as blue glass. 'Sorry enough to accompany me to the hospital tonight?'

She almost said 'The hospital?' before she managed to bite back the fatuous words and say instead, 'Why would you want me to do that, Mr Quentin?' with some modicum of composure.

'I told you, I don't like hospitals,' he said easily as he settled back in the leather seat. 'Besides, I'm sure Madge would feel more comfortable with another woman around.'

'I thought you had a date for tonight? I'm sure Miss de Menthe would be pleased to accompany you.' She hadn't meant to say it but it had just sort of popped out on its own.

'Caroline is not the sort of woman you take to the hospital to visit your aged secretary,' he said drily.

No, she'd just bet she wasn't! Sephy thought nastily. No doubt he had something else entirely in mind for the voluptuous model.

'But of course if you have other plans...'

She stared at him, her mind racing. If she stayed at home she would have to go to the party, and that would mean a night of further embarrassment with Jerry, because one thing was for sure—he'd made up his mind he wasn't going to take no for an answer. Which would have been nice and flattering if she'd even the slightest inkling of ever fancying him. As it was...

'When are you thinking of going?' she asked carefully, her voice low.

'Now seems as good a time as any.' And then he smiled slowly, a fascinatingly breath-stopping smile, as he added, 'Does that mean you are considering taking pity on me?'

Sephy stood as though glued to the hot pavement and swallowed twice before she managed to say, 'I'll have to go and change first. I'll be about five minutes?'

'Fine.' He glanced over her shoulder. 'The guy who isn't the boyfriend looks like he wants a word with you,' he drawled laconically before the sapphire gaze homed in again on her warm face.

'Yes, right...' She was backing away as she spoke, suddenly overwhelmed by what she had agreed to.

She must be mad, she told herself silently as she walked back to Jerry, who was waiting in the doorway of his shop, his pleasant, attractive face straight and his brown eyes fixed on her face. If it was a choice of an evening fending off Jerry as kindly as she could or choosing to spend an hour or so in Conrad Quentin's company there was no contest! The amiable puppy had it every time. But it was too late now.

'You told me your boss was small and fat and had eight grandchildren,' Jerry accused her as she reached his side.

'He is and he does,' Sephy said weakly. 'That's the owner of the business, Mr Quentin, and I'm standing in for his secretary for a while. There...there's an emergency and I've got to go with him.' She was terribly conscious of the parked car behind them.

'Now?' Jerry made no effort to lower his voice.

'I'm afraid so.' She nodded firmly and inserted the key in the lock as she added, 'So it looks like the party is off for me, Jerry. Make my apologies to Maisie, would you? Tell her I'll see her at the weekend. For a coffee or something.'

'How long do you think you will be?' He was nothing if not hopeful, his voice holding a pleading note which increased her guilt.

'Ages,' she answered briskly as the door swung wide. 'Bye, Jerry.' This was definitely a case of being cruel to be kind.

She ran quickly up the stairs to the flat, but once inside in the small neat hall she stopped still, staring at her reflection in the charming antique mirror her mother had bought her for a housewarming present.

Anxious honey-brown eyes stared back at her, and it was their expression she answered as she said, 'You might well be worried! As though working with him isn't bad enough you have to agree to go with him tonight.' He obviously wouldn't have dreamt asking the beautiful Caroline to do anything so mundane, but Sephy Vincent? Well, she was just part of the office machine, there to serve and obey. She grimaced at her reflection irritably.

What had he said? Oh, yes—Caroline de Menthe was

not the sort of woman you took to a hospital to visit your secretary. She—clearly—was. Which said it all, really.

The soft liquid eyes narrowed and hardened and her mouth became tight. Okay, so she wasn't an oil painting and she never would be, and she could do with losing a few pounds too, but no one had ever suggested she walk round with a paper bag over her head! And Jerry fancied her.

The last thought brought her back to earth with a bump. What was she doing feeling sorry for herself? she asked the dark-haired girl in the mirror with something akin to amazement in her face now. This wasn't like her. But then she hadn't felt like herself all afternoon if it came to it. It was him, Conrad Quentin. He was…disturbing. And he was also waiting outside, she reminded herself sharply, diving through to the bedroom in the same instant.

She threw off her crumpled work clothes and grabbed a pretty knee-length flowered skirt she had bought the week before, teaming it with a little white top and matching waist-length cardigan. She didn't have time to shower, she decided feverishly, but she quickly bundled her hair in a high knot on top of her head, teasing her fringe and several tendrils loose, and then applied a touch of eyeshadow and a layer of mascara to widen her eyes.

The whole procedure had taken no more than five minutes and she was out in the street again in six, to find him lying back indolently in the seat with his eyes shut and his hands behind his head as he listened to Frank Sinatra singing about doing it his way.

Very appropriate, she thought a trifle caustically. If only half the stories about Conrad Quentin were true he certainly lived his life by that principle.

His eyes opened as she reached the car and he straightened, glancing at his watch as he murmured, 'When you say five minutes you really mean five minutes, don't you?'

before leaning across and opening the passenger door for her to slide in.

'You find that surprising?' she asked unevenly as the closeness of him registered and all her senses went into hyperdrive.

'For a woman to say what she means?' He half turned in his seat, the brilliant blue gaze raking her hot face. 'More of a minor miracle,' he drawled cynically, one black eyebrow quirking mockingly as he started the engine.

Sephy would have liked to come back with a sharp, clever retort, but the truth of the matter was that she was floundering. She'd never ridden in a Mercedes before for a start, and the big beautiful car was truly gorgeous, but it was the man at the wheel who was really taking her breath away.

The office—with plenty of air space, not to mention desks, chairs and all the other paraphernalia—was one thing; the close confines of the car were quite another. They emphasised his dominating masculinity a hundredfold, and underlined the dark, dangerous quality of his attractiveness enough to have her sitting as rigid as a piece of wood.

She tried telling herself she was stupid and pathetic and ridiculous, but with the faint smell of his aftershave teasing her senses and his body warmth all about her it didn't do any good. This was Conrad Quentin—*Conrad Quentin*—and she still couldn't quite believe the whole afternoon had happened, or that she was actually sitting here with him like this.

She felt a momentary thrill that she didn't understand and that was entirely inappropriate in the circumstances, and reminded herself—sharply now—that she had to keep her wits about her after the episode of the keys if he wasn't going to think she was utterly dense. She was a useful office item as far as he was concerned—like the fax or the computer—and he expected cool, efficient service.

He was a very exacting employer, and it was well known that he suffered fools badly—in fact he didn't suffer them at all! And that was fair enough, she told herself silently, when you considered he paid top salaries with manifold perks like private health insurance and so on.

He was the original work hard and play hard business tycoon, and until today she had never so much as exchanged more than half a dozen words with him, so it wasn't surprising she was feeling a bit…tense. Well, more than a bit, she admitted ruefully.

And then, as though he had read her mind, she was conscious of the hard profile turning her way for an instant before he said softly, 'Relax, Seraphina. I'm not going to eat you.'

Her head shot round, but he was looking straight ahead at the road again and the imperturbable face was expressionless.

It took her a second or two, but then she was able to say, her voice verging on the icy, 'I don't know what you mean, Mr Quentin,' even as she knew her face was burning with hot colour.

'The suggestion that you accompany me to the hospital was purely spontaneous,' he said mildly, without looking at her again. 'I'm not about to leap on you and have my wicked way, if that's what's worrying you.'

'Nothing is worrying me,' she bit back immediately, horrified beyond measure, 'and I wouldn't dream of thinking you intended…that you would even think of—' She stopped abruptly, aware that she was about to burst into flames, and took a deep breath before she said, 'I'm quite sure you are not that sort of man, Mr Quentin.'

There was a moment of blank silence, when Sephy felt the temperature drop about thirty degrees, and then he said, his dark voice silky-soft, 'I do like women, Miss Vincent.'

This was getting worse! 'I know you do,' she said

quickly. 'Of course I know that; everyone does. I just meant—' She wasn't improving matters, she realised suddenly, as she risked a sidelong glance at the cold rugged face.

'Please, do continue.' It was curt and clipped. '"Everyone" takes an interest in my love life, do they?'

Oh, blow it! He was the one prancing about with a different woman each week! What did he expect for goodness' sake? 'I was just trying to say I know you like women, that's all,' Sephy said primly, her face burning with a mixture of embarrassment and disquiet.

'Right. So my sexual persuasion is not in question.' There was liquid ice in his deep voice. 'That taken as read, why would it be so unlikely that I might have ulterior motives in asking you to spend the evening with me?'

The evening? They were going to visit poor Madge Watkins, that was all! Afterwards she would realise she could have answered in a host of ways to defuse what had become an electric moment: he was not the sort of man to mix business and pleasure would have been a good one; she was aware he was dating someone at the moment could have been another. What she did say, the words tumbling out of her mouth, was, 'There has to be some sort of a spark between a man and a woman, doesn't there? And I'm not your type.'

'My *type*?' If she had accused him of a gross obscenity he couldn't have sounded more offended. There was another chilling pause, and then he said, 'What, exactly, do you consider my "type", Miss Vincent?' as he viciously cut up a harmless, peaceable family saloon that had been sailing along minding its own business.

She couldn't make it any worse. She might as well be honest, Sephy told herself silently as the two 'Miss Vincents' after all the 'Seraphinas' of the day registered like the kiss of death on her career. 'Women like Miss de Menthe, I suppose,' she said shakily.

'Meaning?' he queried testily.

He didn't intend to make this easy. 'Beautiful, successful, rich...' Spoilt, selfish, bitchy...

The grooves that splayed out from either side of his nose to his mouth deepened, as though she had actually voiced the last three words, but he remained silent, although it was a silence that vibrated with painful tension. Finally, he said coldly, 'So, we've ascertained my type. What is your type, Seraphina?'

At least the Seraphina was back, although she didn't know if that was a good or a bad thing, Sephy thought feverishly as she clasped her hands together so tightly the knuckles showed white. And her *type*? That was funny if he did but know it. In the age of the Pill and condoms being bought as casually as bunches of flowers, she must be the only girl in the whole of London whose sexual experience was minimal to say the least. But that was the last thing she could say to a man of the world like Conrad Quentin. He'd laugh his head off.

The thought brought the door in her mind behind which she kept the caustic memories of the past slightly ajar, and as the image of David intruded for a second her stomach turned over. And then she had slammed it shut again, her mouth tightening as she willed the humiliation and pain to die.

She forced herself to shrug easily and kept her voice light as she said, 'I guess I'm not fussy on looks; dark or fair, tall or short, it doesn't matter as long as the guy is a nice person.'

'A nice person?' he returned mockingly, with a lift of one dark eyebrow, his large capable hands firmly on the wheel as he executed a manoeuvre that Sephy knew wasn't exactly legal, and which caused a medley of car horns to blare behind them as the Mercedes dived off into a side-street to avoid the traffic jam which had been ahead. 'And how would you define a nice person?'

A man who could accept that one-night stands and casual sex weren't obligatory on the first date? Someone who could understand that some women—or certainly this one at least—needed to be in love before they would allow full intimacy, and who was prepared to think with his head and hopefully his heart rather than that other vital organ some inches lower. Someone who cared about her just a little more than their own ego, who didn't mind that she hadn't got a perfect thirty-six, twenty-four, thirty-six figure, with fluffy blonde hair and big blue eyes, someone...someone from her dreams.

Sephy twisted in the seat, knowing she had to say something, and then managed, 'A man who is kind and funny and gentle, I suppose,' and then cringed inside as he snorted mockingly.

'And that's it?' he asked scathingly. 'You don't want a man, Seraphina. Your average cocker spaniel would do just as well. And the lovelorn guy back at your flat, does he fit all the criteria?' he added before she could react to the acidic sarcasm.

'Jerry?' she asked with a stiffness that should have warned him.

'Is that his name?' He couldn't have sounded more derisory if she'd said Donald Duck. 'Well, it's clear Jerry's got it bad, and he looked a fine, upstanding pillar of the establishment and *impossibly* kind and gentle, or am I wrong?'

She didn't often get angry, but around this man she seemed to be little else, and now the words were on her tongue without her even having to think about them. 'I wasn't aware that my job description necessitated talking about my friends,' she said with savage coldness, 'but if it

does you had better accept my resignation here and now,
Mr Quentin.'

There was absolute silence for a screaming moment, but
as Sephy glared at him the cool profile was magnificently
indifferent. He'd make a fantastic poker player, she thought
irrelevantly. No wonder he was so formidable in business.

'The name's Conrad.'

'What?' If he had taken all his clothes off and danced
stark naked on the Mercedes' beautiful leather seats she
couldn't have been more taken aback.

'I said, the name is Conrad,' he said evenly, without
taking his eyes from the view beyond the car's bonnet. 'If
we are going to be working together for some weeks I can't
be doing with Mr Quentin this and Mr Quentin that; it's
irritating in the extreme.'

She wanted—she did so *want*—to be able to match him
for cool aplomb and control, but it was a lost cause, she
acknowledged weakly as she sank back in her seat without
saying another word. Game, set and match to him, the in-
sensitive, cold-blooded, arrogant so-and-so.

CHAPTER THREE

THEY stopped on the way to buy flowers and chocolates for Madge—the flowers taking up the whole of the back seat of the car and the box of chocolates large enough to feed a hundred little old ladies for a week—and it was just after half past seven when the Mercedes nosed its way into the immaculate car park of the small, select private hospital on the outskirts of Harlow.

The dusky shadowed twilight carried the scent of the crisply cut lawns which surrounded the gracious building, and as Sephy nervously accompanied Conrad up the wide, horseshoe-shaped stone steps to the front door, her arms laden with flowers, the surrealness of it all was making her light-headed.

If anyone had told her that morning she would be spending part of the evening in the company of the exalted head of Quentin Dynamics she would have laughed in their face, but here she was. And here he was. All six foot plus of him.

She darted a glance from under her eyelashes at the tall, dark figure next to her and her heart gave a little jump. He exuded maleness. It was there in every line of the lean powerful body and hard chiselled face, and as her female hormones seemed horribly determined to react—with a life all of their own—to his own particular brand of virile masculinity it didn't make for easy companionship.

Once they were inside the building the attractive, red-haired receptionist nearly fell over herself to escort them to Madge's room, which—as Conrad had decreed—was the best in the place.

But Sephy didn't notice the ankle-deep carpeting, exclusive and beautifully co-ordinated furnishings or the magnificent view from the large bay window over the lawns and trees surrounding the hospital. All her attention was taken up with the fragile, pathetic little figure huddled in the bed.

At a little over four foot ten Madge Watkins had always been tiny, but she seemed to have shrunk down to nothing since the day before and the effect was shocking.

Her grey hair looked limp and scanty, her skin was a pasty white colour, and the expression in her faded blue eyes stated quite clearly she was terrified. Sephy's heart went out to her.

So, apparently, did Conrad's.

The aggressive and ruthless tycoon of working hours and the mocking, contemptuous escort of the last forty-five minutes or so metamorphosed into someone Sephy didn't recognise. He was quiet and tender with his elderly secretary, dumping the chocolates and the rest of the flowers he was carrying on a chair, before taking the shrivelled thin figure in his arms and holding her close for long moments without speaking.

Madge's face was wet by the time he settled her back against her pillows, but then he sat by her side, talking soothingly and positively after he had drawn Sephy forward to make her greetings. After a while it dawned on Sephy that Conrad and his secretary had a very special relationship—more like mother and son than boss and employee. And it stunned her. Totally.

The receptionist brought them all tea and cakes at just after eight o'clock, and by the time they left, at ten to nine, Madge was smiling and conversing quite naturally, the look of stark dread gone from her eyes and her face animated.

'You needn't come again, lad.'

Once Madge had relaxed and understood Conrad had no

intention of standing on ceremony in front of Sephy, she had referred to her brilliant boss as 'lad' a few times, and Sephy had realised that the special circumstances were allowing her to see the way they were normally when they were alone. Before this night she had never heard Madge give him anything but his full title, and even at the Christmas dances and such the elderly woman had always been extremely stiff and proper.

'Of course I'm coming again, woman!' His voice was rough but his face was something else as he glanced at the small figure in the bed, and Sephy was surprised at the jolt her heart gave.

'No, really, lad. I know how you hate these places,' Madge said earnestly.

And then she stopped speaking as Conrad laid his hand over her scrawny ones and said very softly, 'I said I'll be back, Madge. Now, then, no more of that. And you're not rushing home to that empty house before you're able to look after yourself either. You're going to get better, the doctor's assured me about that, but it'll take time and you'll have to be patient for once in your life.'

'There's the pot calling the kettle,' Madge said weakly, her eyes swimming with tears again as his concern and love touched her.

It touched Sephy too, but in her case the overwhelming feeling was one of confusion and agitation and the knowledge that it had been a mistake—a big, big mistake—to come here with him like this. As the cold, ruthless, cynical potentate Conrad Quentin was someone she disliked, as the ladykiller and rake he was someone she despised, and as her temporary boss he was someone she respected, for his incredibly intelligent mind and the rapier-sharp acumen that was mind-blowing, at the same time as feeling an aversion for such cold, obsessional single-mindedness.

But tonight... How did she think about him tonight? she

asked herself nervously as she watched him make his good-byes to Madge. But, no, he was her boss—just her boss—and come tomorrow morning things would be back on a more formal footing and she would forget how she was feeling right now—she *would*; of course she would! She, of all people, knew that men like him—wildly attractive, charismatic brutes of men—were shallow and egocentric and could charm the birds out of the trees when they liked.

They had just reached the door when Madge's voice, urgent and high, brought them turning to face her again. 'Angus! I forgot about Angus. I can't believe I could forget him. He's had no dinner, Conrad.'

'He could live on his fat for years, Madge, so don't put on sackcloth and ashes,' Conrad said drily, and in answer to Sephy's enquiring face he added, 'Madge's cat,' by way of explanation.

'He'll be wondering where I am—'

'Don't worry.' Conrad cut short Madge's tremulous voice, his own resigned. 'I'll pick him up on the way home and he can board with me for a while until you're home again. Daniella loves cats, as you know—even Angus. She'll look after him.'

Daniella? Who was Daniella? And then a prim voice in her head admonished, It's nothing to do with you who Daniella is.

It was dark outside, the air a wonderful scented mixture of grass and woodsmoke and hot summer days after the sterile warmth of the hospital, and Sephy raised her head as she took several deep gulps of the intoxicating mixture.

'Thanks, Sephy.' His voice was unusually soft.

Surprised into looking at him, she became aware he was watching her closely from narrowed blue eyes, his hands thrust deep in his pockets and the brooding quality she had noticed about him more than once very evident.

'Sephy?' She stared at him, suddenly acutely shy without knowing why. 'You said you didn't intend to call me that.'

'It seems the least I can do after you've helped me out so ungrudgingly this evening,' he said with quiet sincerity.

It made her previous thoughts about him uncharitable, to say the least, and she could feel herself blushing as she said, 'That's all right; it killed two birds with one stone, actually.'

'Yes?' He glanced down enquiringly as they began to walk.

'I'd been invited to a party that I didn't want to go to but it would have been difficult to get out of it without a valid excuse,' she explained quietly.

'And there was me thinking you had succumbed to my irresistible charm.'

It was cool and light, but somehow she got the impression he wasn't as amused as his smile would have liked her to believe, and something he had said earlier in the day—'many a true word is spoken in jest'—came back to her. The male ego again. She mentally nodded at the thought. The male sex in general really did seem to believe they had been put on the earth to receive due homage.

'Anyway, party or no, the least I can do is to feed you before I take you back,' he said smoothly, for all the world as though she was a little lost orphan he had found wandering about the streets of London. 'Come on, we'll stop off for a bite to eat on the way home. I know I'm starving.'

She stared at him uncertainly, searching for the right words to refuse his invitation without appearing rude. Dinner with Conrad Quentin? She wouldn't be able to eat a thing, she told herself feverishly as she stopped dead in her tracks. 'But...'

'Yes?' He glanced down at her again and his eyes were cool.

'What about Miss de Menthe?' she said quickly. 'I thought you were seeing her tonight?'

'Cancelled,' he said cryptically.

'And there's Madge's cat.' Thank goodness for Madge's cat.

'So there is.' His gaze was distinctly cold now, and when she still didn't move he made a quiet sound of annoyance and took her arm in one firm hand, guiding her along the winding path between bowling-green-smooth stretches of grass and into the car park.

His flesh was warm through the thin cotton of her cardigan, and it wasn't the swiftness with which he was urging her along that made her suddenly short of breath. He was so big, so male, so much of everything if the truth be known. And knowing what he was like, all the women he had had, made her feel gauche and inadequate and totally out of her depth. He smelt absolutely wonderful. The unwelcome intrusion of the thought did nothing to calm the wild flutters of panic that were turning her stomach upside down.

He opened the car door for her when they reached the Mercedes, and as he leant over her slightly it took every ounce of her will-power to slide into the confines of the car with a small polite nod of her head, as though she was totally oblivious to his male warmth.

And then, as he walked lazily round the bonnet of the car, she took herself severely in hand. Conrad Quentin was one of those men who had everything—wealth, success and an alarming amount of sex appeal—and she'd better get it clear in her head now that she wasn't going to let him intimidate her, consciously or unconsciously. If she was going to continue standing in for Madge, that was. Which she rather thought she was, crazy though that made her. Anyway, she had given him her word at the office earlier, so that was that. She couldn't back out now.

'You're frowning.'

She glanced up to see a pair of very piercing blue eyes surveying her through the open driver's door, and then, as she flushed hotly, he slid into the seat and started the engine with a flick of his hand.

Sephy waited for him to follow up on his terse statement, but when they had gone a mile or two and he still hadn't spoken she swallowed drily, and then said quietly, 'Mr Quentin—'

'Conrad,' he interrupted pleasantly.

She tried to ignore the long lean legs stretched out under the steering wheel and the delicious faint odour of what must be wildly expensive aftershave, and took another surreptitious swallow before she managed, 'Conrad, there really is no need to buy me dinner. I'm sure you must be terribly busy, and I've masses of things to do when I get home—'

'Don't you want to have dinner with me, Sephy?' he interrupted again, the even tone fooling her not at all.

She hesitated just a second too long before she said, 'It's not that. Of course it's not that I don't *want* to.'

'No?' It was very dry. 'Well, we won't labour the point. I take it you have no objection in calling in Madge's place on the way back and picking up the terrible Angus? It is *en route*, so it makes sense.'

She wanted to ask, Why the *terrible* Angus? but said instead, 'Yes, of course. That's fine,' her voice tight and stiff.

'And it might be easier to drop him off at my house before I take you home; he doesn't like travelling and it'll be less stressful,' he continued smoothly. 'We don't want to distress him.'

Put like that, she could hardly do anything else but agree. She had no idea where he lived, but somehow she didn't feel she could ask him either. She just hoped it wasn't *too* far from Madge's.

Madge's house turned out to be a small and awe-inspiringly neat semi in Epping, with a paved front garden methodically interspersed with miniature shrubs. The interior of the building smelt of mothballs and furniture polish and was as spick and span as the front garden. It was *exactly* Madge—which made Angus all the more of a shock.

The cat was an enormous battle-scarred ginger tom, with a shredded right ear, a twisted tail that looked distinctly the worse for wear and a blemished nose that bore evidence of numerous fights. He was the very antithesis of what Sephy had expected.

He was waiting for them in Madge's gleaming compact little kitchen when Conrad opened the door from the hall, which had been firmly closed, and it was clear he was confined to that room of the house during the working day from the massive cat flap in the back door, which gave him access to the rear garden, and the big, warm comfortable basket in one corner of the kitchen, next to which were two saucers. Two *empty* saucers—a fact which the cat immediately brought to their attention by his plaintive miaows.

'Oh, he must be starving, poor thing.'

Sephy was all concern as the enormous feline wound hopefully round her legs, but as she glanced anxiously at Conrad she saw him shake his head mockingly, and his voice was amused as he said, 'He'd have you wrapped round one paw the same as he has Madge. If ever a cat could look after itself this one can, I assure you. Angus always has his eye to the main chance and he keeps everyone dancing to his tune.'

It takes one to recognise one.

For an awful moment Sephy thought she had actually spoken the words out loud, but when Conrad's face didn't change and he merely gathered up the cat basket and the saucers she breathed out a silent sigh of relief. She'd said more than enough already.

'See if you can find a tin of cat food for tonight while I take these out to the car. Although once I get him home I dare say Daniella will be feeding him salmon and steak.' Conrad shook his head again at the huge cat, who eyed him unblinkingly out of serene emerald eyes. 'He boarded with us last year while Madge had a couple of weeks' holiday with her sister, and he didn't taste cat food once.'

'Daniella?' Sephy queried carefully as he passed her with the basket. She didn't think it unreasonable to ask now.

'My housekeeper,' he tossed easily over his shoulder.

His housekeeper. As the kitchen door closed behind him Sephy stood staring into space as she pictured a nice, plump, middle-aged little body, and then, as she heard Conrad returning, quickly opened a cupboard or two for the supply of cat food.

Angus submitted perfectly happily to being carried out to the car, his two huge front paws resting on Conrad's chest as he gazed solemnly at Sephy over Conrad's shoulder when she followed them out. Once in the Mercedes, however, the calm composure faltered a bit as he crouched on the back seat and began to growl as Conrad started the engine. A low, heated and rather nasty growl.

'Ignore him.' Conrad appeared quite unconcerned. 'He'll keep that up until we reach home, but as long as he isn't confined that's all he'll do. He just hates being shut in.'

'How do you know that?' Sephy asked nervously. The animal was half domestic cat, half lion, and she didn't fancy having those vicious claws and teeth in the back of her neck.

'Because I made the mistake of putting him in a cat carrier Madge had provided the last time,' Conrad said evenly, his face expressionless. 'It's called learning the hard way.'

'Bad idea?'

'You could say that.' It was clear the subject wasn't a favourite one. 'He'd ripped it apart and escaped before we were halfway home, and he leapt about the car like a demoniac maniac before he decided to take his revenge by scenting every corner.'

'Oh, I see.' The mental picture of her suave, cool, imperturbable boss being put in his place so completely by a cat was sweet, and although she managed to keep her face straight there was a gurgle of laughter in her voice as she said, 'He's a big cat.'

'With a big bladder.' The blue eyes raked her face for one moment. 'I had the car cleaned three times before I got rid of the odour, and even then the smell wafted back on hot days.'

She glanced round at Angus, who was sitting quite quietly apart from the low, threatening growl in the back of his throat, and as honey-brown eyes met brilliant green she could have sworn the cat winked at her. She smiled at him, she couldn't help it, and then turned back in her seat again, her eyes scanning the hard male profile at the side of her as she did so. The amusement left her features abruptly.

Somehow she was more entangled in Conrad Quentin's life after a few hours than she was in Mr Harper's after working for him for a few years. She didn't quite know how it had happened, but something was telling her it was unwise at best, and at worst it was downright dangerous. He had something, a drawing power, a magnetism, and how was she going to feel when Madge was back at work and she was unceremoniously dumped back into Customer Services? But that was stupid—she'd feel relieved. Of course she would.

'My house is on the outskirts of Edgware.' His voice, calm and controlled and even as always, cut in on her racing thoughts. 'And I do appreciate you helping me out like this, Sephy.'

The charm was out in full force, she thought with unusual cynicism, but then as she was complying with that determined, hard male will perhaps it wasn't surprising. He was a man who didn't like to be crossed, even in the smallest of things. 'No problem. No problem at all,' she said lightly, glancing out of the side window at the dark, shadowed road along which they were travelling. 'Like I said, this has done me a favour in a way.'

'Ah, yes, the party.' There was a granite quality to his voice for a moment, and then it cleared as he said silkily, 'This might surprise you but I don't usually have to try and persuade a woman to spend time in my company, not since I made my first million anyway. And I can't remember one refusing dinner before.'

She said nothing, simply because she couldn't think of anything which would defuse what had suddenly become an electric moment.

'This Jerry—do you intend to put the poor man out of his misery and go out with him, or is there someone else on the horizon?' he asked conversationally, so conversationally she felt she couldn't really ask him to mind his own business, as she would have liked to do and as she felt he deserved.

'No to both,' she answered shortly, hoping he would take the hint.

He didn't. 'So you're fancy-free and single?' he drawled easily. 'Enjoying the odd date but without any ties or commitments?' He didn't look at her as he spoke, his eyes on the windscreen.

'There hasn't been an "odd date" for quite some time.' She aimed to make her voice faintly amused, as though she wasn't as taut as piano wire inside. 'But, yes, I suppose you could put it like that.' Not that my private life is anything to do with you.

He nodded slowly. 'Are you a career girl?' he asked evenly.

Bearing in mind who he was, she could really only answer in one way, but it had the added advantage of being the truth when she said, 'Yes, I am, if being a career girl means I want to do well in my job and get somewhere.'

'And you enjoy being independent and autonomous.' This time it was a statement, and Sephy stiffened slightly. He saw too much, this man, and she didn't like where the conversation was going.

She forced herself to take a deep calming breath before she shrugged and said airily, 'Doesn't everyone at some stage?'

'No, I don't think so,' he challenged smoothly.

'Well, most of my friends think that way.' Her voice was too defensive, and she recognised it even before he spoke.

'I'm sorry, I seem to have touched a nerve,' he said, in a voice which suggested he wasn't sorry at all.

Arrogant swine! She gritted her teeth and stared straight ahead.

The rest of the journey was conducted in a silence in which Conrad seemed to feel extremely comfortable but which Sephy found unpleasant and disturbing to say the least. It didn't help that he was completely oblivious to her and she was aware of every tiny movement he made—his strong capable hands on the wheel, his big powerful body, the way his trousers pulled tight over lean thighs...

Sexual attraction. The words were stark but Sephy faced them bravely, aware she had been putting off the moment all day. Okay, so she was sexually attracted to him and she hadn't felt this way in years, not since... Her thought process hesitated, and then she followed through. Not since David.

David Bainbridge. The cliché of tall, dark and handsome. He had been the ultimate prize in the small village community near Banbury where she had been born, and the summer after she had finished her A levels and he had been home on holiday from university had been a thrilling one.

His father was something big in the City, and from the age of seventeen David had driven his own red sports car with a different girl in tow for every day of the week. Sephy had always been in awe of him, and consequently excruciatingly shy in his presence whenever the young people of the villages thereabouts got together. Her shyness had expressed itself in a cool aloofness that had earned her the nickname 'Ice Maiden' amongst the lads, although she hadn't known about that at the time.

She had been a short fat toddler and a short fat child, and even at eighteen a vestige of puppy fat had remained. That, combined with her abundance of freckles and the ugly brace she had had to wear on her teeth, had made her self-esteem zero, but she had hidden her lack of confidence under a reserved, touch-me-not exterior that protected the vulnerable girl underneath.

And then that summer David had appeared interested in her. He had returned from university with a beautiful blonde who had stayed two weeks and then disappeared to visit her family in Sweden, and from almost the day Annika had left David had begun seeking her out at the local dances, picnics, visits to the pub and so on. He had been quite open about it.

She hadn't been able to believe it at first, and then she had floated in a bubble of wonder and excitement as she had waited for him to ask her for a date, a real date, without any of the rest of the crowd along. She had dreamt about the moment for nights on end.

And then he had asked, one evening when a gang of them had been sipping ice-cold beer in the garden of the village pub. David had taken her aside and told her he was crazy about her, that he couldn't understand how he'd never noticed her before, that he really wanted them to get to know each other better.

'Come for a quiet meal at my place?' he suggested softly, his arms round her waist and his ebony eyes looking into her dazed brown ones. 'The parents are away so we'll have the house to ourselves. We can get a video and just chill out with a pizza and a bottle of wine. Please, Sephy?'

And he kissed her, drawing her into him as his hands moved seductively over her body before wandering under the loose thin cotton top she had on and cradling her breasts, his thumbs rubbing and tweaking their hard points until she thought she'd melt right at his feet.

It was her first kiss, her first tentative sexual encounter, and it blew her mind. She had worshipped him from afar all her life and suddenly the impossible, the *inconceivable* was happening. He'd fallen for her. *Her...*

She was the girl he drove home in his flash red sports car that night, and as they waved goodbye to the others she felt as though she was in a wonderful, blissful dream.

And then the dream turned into a nightmare.

It was her friend Glenis who told her. Glenis came round the next morning, sympathetic and commiserating but with an edge to her pity that told Sephy the other girl was perhaps secretly relishing the drama too, to say that Robbie— Glenis's boyfriend—had told her on the quiet that David was taking Sephy out for a bet.

'A bet?' Sephy looked into Glenis's round eyes, owl-like behind their thick glasses. 'I don't understand.'

Glenis wriggled a bit, but she still took a delight in telling her. 'One of the lads, I don't know who, bet David that he couldn't get the ''Ice-Maiden''—that's you—into bed on a first date,' Glenis said conspiratorially. 'And David said he could. His parents are away in America for a few weeks so he told the lads he'd do it at his house, and they could hide in a spare bedroom and then he'd call them in to prove it when he'd finished. I'm sorry, Sephy, but I couldn't let you walk into that, could I? I had to tell you. I couldn't believe it at first, but it is true, honest.'

She thanked Glenis somehow, and once the other girl had gone picked up the telephone with numb fingers and called David's home. She didn't think about what to say, she just asked him. And he didn't even try to pretend once he knew he had been rumbled. That hurt as much as anything else. He was offhand and contemptuous and amused, and it was he who put the phone down on her.

She wanted to die for a time, dragging herself through each day and putting up a front whenever she was with the others until her nerves were as raw and lacerated as her heart. And at the bottom of her, whatever she tried to tell herself through the long sleepless nights when she tossed and turned until she thought she'd go mad, she knew David would have won his bet if she had gone to his home that night. She had been his for the taking and he had known it. Known she was crazy about him, that she adored him.

And then the holidays finished and David and some of the others went back to university. Months passed and she had the brace off and learnt to make the best of her naturally thick silky hair and smooth creamy skin; several hours at the gym each week toned her body and improved her shape. She took a college course in business management and secretarial skills, and, armed with that and her excellent A levels, left the womb-like village life and her mother's small, pretty cottage and headed for London at the age of twenty.

But somehow, deep inside, she was still that small, hurt, shy teenager who had had the ground swept from under her feet and had been left vulnerable and exposed, and she had never fully realised it until this moment. She had carved a new life for herself, even dated occasionally—never the same man twice and always allowing nothing more than a goodnight kiss, although most of them had seemed to think ending up in bed was a good idea—and she'd become adept and composed at handling all of life's ups and downs. And yet sexually and emotionally she had frozen that morning in front of Glenis, and it could have been yesterday so securely had the ice held.

And then this morning she had been drawn into Conrad Quentin's fiery orbit and now the ice was melting. She was attracted to him. She didn't want to be, but she didn't seem able to control the feeling. And he was just another David at heart. Oh, he was undoubtedly wealthier, more powerful, more magnetic and fascinating, but basically he was a ruthless womaniser who worked hard and played hard and lived his life by his own set of rules.

Was she one of those women she'd read about? she asked herself searchingly. Women with a built-in self-destruct button who were always drawn to men who would use and abuse them; men who were charming and hypnotic but with a flaw that made them cruelly self-absorbed and narcissistic?

But, no, any woman would be attracted to Conrad Quentin; he was extremely fanciable, she reassured herself in the next moment. This was just a lust thing, however you wanted to dress it up, an animal awareness, something base and carnal, and as such quite easily controlled once it had been recognised.

And as she was as far out of his league of beautiful, famous models and starlets and the like as the man in the moon, it really didn't matter too much one way or the other anyway. Conrad Quentin would never bother with someone like her—why, she'd worked for Quentin Dynamics for six years and he hadn't even known she'd existed until fate had put her right under his nose!

Sephy had been lost in her dark thoughts and oblivious to the miles the powerful car had eaten up, so now, as a deep, husky voice at the side of her said quietly, 'Here we are. Angus will soon be in Daniella's tender care,' she raised her head in startled surprise to see the car was pulling up in front of a nine-foot-high security wall with massive gates set in it, which Conrad opened smoothly with remote control from the car.

Once through the gates, the car moved slowly along a curved, pebble-covered driveway which opened on to a wide sweep in front of a very gracious, large, red-roofed house. Immaculate bowling-green-flat lawns surrounded the mansion on three sides, with a border of mature trees and bushes hiding the wall from view, and at their approach security lights lit up the grounds as bright as day.

It was all very epicurean and controlled—just like Conrad Quentin—and the beautifully tended gardens and rich scents coming from the warm vegetation suggested they were in the middle of the country somewhere, rather than the city. A lavish, opulent, fertile oasis in the middle of a desert of high-rise buildings and the madness of the rat-race, Sephy thought enviously. How the other half lived!

Conrad had left the car and walked round to open her door whilst she had been gaping at the view, and now, as his warm hand cupped her elbow once she was standing on the drive, he said, 'Come in and have a drink while you're here.'

'Angus...' She gestured somewhat vacantly towards the parked Mercedes' back seat, only to turn her head again and see one very dignified, massive ginger tom padding ahead of them towards the house, his tail straight up in the air and every line of his body indicating he wanted it made plain he was doing Conrad the most enormous favour by consenting to be his guest.

'He knows the way,' Conrad said wryly. 'I told you, you needn't concern yourself about him. He's streetwise.'

It wasn't the cat that was worrying her, Sephy thought with a touch of silent hysteria as she allowed herself to be ushered through the huge double front doors and into a truly baronial hall that would have swallowed her little flat whole. She had a fleetingly brief impression of dark gleaming wood, bowls of flowers and undeniably fine paintings before she found herself entering what was clearly the drawing room. Just as she sank down on the silk-covered chaise longue Conrad indicated, a slender, dark-haired and exquisitely lovely young woman followed them into the room. The girl was holding Angus in her arms and the big cat was purring loudly.

'He is telling me he wants his dinner,' the woman said laughingly in a bright, heavily accented voice, glancing at Conrad as she spoke. Then she turned to Sephy and added, 'You must be Sephy, yes? I am Daniella and I am pleasured to meet you,' adjusting Angus in her arms so she could shake Sephy's hand.

'You are *pleased* to meet her,' Conrad corrected softly with an indulgent smile. 'And I brought a tin of cat food from Madge's, incidentally, until you can get some tomorrow.'

'Cat food?' Daniella wrinkled her small perfect nose in utter distaste, turning to Sephy as though for moral support when she said, 'Angus the cat, he no like the food from tins.'

'Not when he can dine on best salmon,' Conrad agreed drily.

'Oh, you! You have the—how do you say it?—the bark that is worse than the bite?' Daniella's voice was warm and loving, and the glance she gave Conrad caused Sephy's eyes to open wide for an instant.

Housekeeper, my foot, she thought balefully. This definitely was no employer/employee relationship, but then she shouldn't really be surprised, should she? It was the nature of the animal after all. But didn't Daniella mind when he paraded women like the lovely Caroline de Menthe in front of her? Obviously not.

'I go now and see to the dinner.'

Daniella was smiling at her, and Sephy could do no more than smile back before she said, 'I'm sure Angus will appreciate that.'

'*Si, si.* I think so too.' And then, as the cat wriggled in her arms, Daniella said, 'Oh, you cat, you are the impatient one,' before she nodded and smiled at them both again. She left the room saying, 'Ten minutes, Conrad? *Si?*'

'Ten minutes will be fine, Daniella. That will give us a chance to have a drink first,' he said with suspicious satisfaction.

'First?' As the door closed behind the young Italian woman Sephy forced herself to speak quietly and calmly, even though her heart was pounding. Something was afoot, she could sense it. 'What does "first" mean?'

'Before something or someone else?' Conrad suggested helpfully as he walked over to a large cocktail cabinet set at the side of a huge bay window and gestured at the bottles that were revealed as he opened the polished wood doors. 'What would you like to drink? Wine? Martini? Or perhaps a gin and tonic?'

'I didn't mean I wanted a dictionary definition,' Sephy said steadily as she met the brilliant blue eyes without flinching. 'And I don't want a drink, thank you.'

He looked at her quietly for a moment. 'Why so wary and guarded, Sephy?' he asked softly. 'Whatever have you heard about me that's so terrible it's scared you to death?'

Sephy's face was brilliant and her voice was sharp with embarrassment as she said, 'I'm not scared! Of course I'm not scared. That's…that's a perfectly ridiculous thing to say.'

'Then you've no objection to staying for dinner?'

She stared at him, her soft golden-brown eyes enormous. Why was it that every conversation with this man was like a minefield? He was manipulative and devious, and he never missed a chance to go for the jugular. It might make him a force to be reckoned with in the business world, but on a personal level she found his high-handedness distinctly offensive. And nerve-racking.

And then, as a thought occurred to her, she said tightly, 'Just now, when Daniella said about seeing to the dinner, she wasn't just talking about Angus's dinner, was she?'

His eyes narrowed just the slightest at her tone but his voice was cool and unconcerned. 'No, she wasn't,' he agreed easily. 'You seemed reluctant to go out for something to eat so I phoned Daniella when I was outside Madge's and asked her to prepare something here for us. But first a drink to clear the palate.'

She might have known! She opened her mouth to object but he was already saying, as he poured two glasses of white wine, 'You have been great tonight, Sephy, and dinner seemed like the least I could do. Added to which, I am, quite frankly, starving. I forgot to eat lunch and breakfast seems like a year ago. Once we have eaten I'll take you straight home, okay?'

He walked across the room and handed her an enormous glass of sparkling white wine with the lazy smile she had seen once or twice, and although she felt as though she had been railroaded Sephy took it with a polite nod of thanks. This was a *fait accompli*. She could do nothing about it so she might as well accept it with good grace. Besides which, being fed and watered was hardly something to complain about. At least it wouldn't be with anyone else!

'Thank you.' She managed to sound courteous without

being deferential. 'But I hope it hasn't put Daniella to a lot of trouble to have to prepare a meal so unexpectedly.'

'She's half-Italian; she loves cooking whatever the time of day,' he said smoothly. 'It's in the genes.'

It might well be, but she just bet he hadn't employed the lovely Italian girl for her culinary skills, Sephy thought with an acid bitterness that shocked her. She'd have to watch herself round this man, she warned herself silently. She was getting crabby and it didn't suit her. She had always prided herself on her sense of humour and tolerant flexibility, and both seemed to have deserted her since she had walked into Conrad Quentin's office.

He sat down opposite her, and although there was a good three feet of space between them her heart started to thunder as he casually crossed one leg over his knee and settled himself more comfortably in the seat. He had discarded his suit jacket as they had walked in the room, slinging it down in a chair, and now, as he placed his wine glass on a small occasional table at the side of him and leant back with his hands clasped behind his head, she caught the dark shadow of body hair beneath the thin silk of his shirt and her mouth went dry. His masculinity was bold and blatant, and all the more threatening for its casual unconsciousness.

He wouldn't know what it was to have to try and pursue a woman, she thought wryly. All he'd have to do was crook his little finger and they would fall into his hands like ripe peaches. Look at Daniella; she was stunning. And there was Caroline de Menthe champing at the bit, and probably others besides for all she knew. They obviously didn't mind that they didn't have the monopoly on his heart or his body; free spirits one and all.

'You're frowning again.'

Her eyes shot to meet his and she saw he was studying her with an air of controlled irritation.

This time she refused to blush and her chin went up a notch as she said coolly, 'I'm sorry.'

'No, you're not,' he said silkily. And then he suddenly leant forward, his elbows resting on his knees as he looked straight into her startled eyes and said softly, 'You disapprove of me, don't you, my stern little secretary with the golden eyes? Who do you get your colouring from? Your father or your mother?'

His voice was smoky, and she rather suspected it was amusement she could hear in its husky depths. The realisation she was being laughed at made her tone brittle when she said, 'Neither, actually. My father was a blue-eyed blond, and my mother's a redhead with hazel eyes.'

'Was?' The amusement was gone and his tone was gentle.

'My father died when I was a baby,' she said shortly.

'I'm sorry.' He actually sounded as though he was. 'And did your mother marry again?'

'No.' She'd never been sure if she was pleased or disappointed about that. It had meant she had had her mother all to herself—she had been their first child—and consequently the two of them were best friends as well as mother and daughter, but she hadn't come into contact with many males during her formative years and it made her a sitting target for someone like David.

'Your mother must have struggled to raise you on her own?' It was another probing question, but spoken as it was, in a quiet, almost tender tone, it didn't occur to her not to answer.

'I suppose so, certainly at first, although our house was paid for on my father's death and he'd had the foresight to take out insurance policies and so on. Once I was at school my mother went to work again—she's a nurse—and she has worked ever since. She likes it. She's risen to the top of her profession now,' she added quietly. 'And no one deserves success more than she does.'

'You're proud of her,' he murmured softly. 'You obviously love her very much.'

'Yes, I do.' She had flushed again and her voice was somewhat defensive. There had been something in his tone she couldn't place, but whatever it was, she didn't like it. 'But it's not unusual to love one's parents, is it?' she added reasonably.

'I wouldn't know. I never had any.' He had risen abruptly as he spoke, and now he held out a hand and said coolly, 'Let me get you another drink.'

She hadn't noticed she had almost drained the glass, but the frantic little sips she had taken in between speaking had all added up, and now she passed him the glass silently, her mind racing. What had he meant, he hadn't had any? Leaving aside the biological necessity, most children who lost their parents were fostered or adopted, surely? If he *had* lost his, that was.

She hesitated, gnawing on the soft underside of her bottom lip, but in view of his pertinent enquiries she felt emboldened to say, as he walked back across the room with her glass, now refilled, 'What do you mean, you never had any?'

For a moment, as she took the proffered glass, she thought from the look on his face he was going to tell her to mind her own business, but instead he expelled a quiet breath and said, his voice cold and expressionless, 'I've always disagreed with the accepted definition of parent. It's clarified as "one who has begotten or borne offspring, father or mother", did you know that? But parenting means much more than that if it's done properly.'

She stared at him, and he stared back at her from vivid blue eyes that were as cold as ice, then moved to lean against the ornate mantelpiece a few feet away. After folding his arms across his chest, he said, his voice taking on an almost bored, flat tone, 'I was born to two human beings, that's all. They had already produced another child, a girl, ten years before, and she had been a mistake too.'

He stopped, as though waiting for her to make some comment, and when she didn't he continued, 'My sister escaped at the age of eighteen by running away, far away, and getting married. And then she returned five years later, to make her peace with our parents, and in a cruel twist of fate which I've never understood she was killed, along with them, when the car they were travelling in from the airport crashed. I was thirteen years old.'

'I'm sorry.' She didn't know what else to say.

He smiled mirthlessly. 'It was a one-day wonder in the newspapers—"Tragic family ripped apart in horror crash" was how it was portrayed—but we were never a family in even the remotest sense of the word. Still, it probably sold a few more papers.'

'What happened to you?' Sephy asked softly. 'Who looked after you?'

'I was at boarding school when it happened and I stayed on, so it was only the holidays when I was passed round the relatives,' he said flatly. 'Looking back, I put them through it. I wasn't nice to be around. I was full of anger and resentment and I let it show. Once I was eighteen and I could claim what was left of my parents' estate after the school, the lawyers, and of course my dear relations had had their pickings for their dubious protection, I took off to see a bit of the world. Bummed around once the money was gone; got into trouble a few times; the usual.'

There was nothing usual about this man, Sephy told herself silently. If nothing else that much was certain.

'And then I woke up one day in some seedy hotel room in Brazil and realised I'd had enough.' A muscle clenched in his hard jaw. 'I couldn't remember anything of the night before and I found I didn't recognise the lady.' The last was very dry. 'So I came back to England and became a respectable member of the establishment...once I'd made my first million, of course. Doors open and memories are very forgiving once you've made your first million.'

'You're very cynical,' she said quietly.

'I'm very practical,' he countered evenly. 'I know that filthy lucre buys anything and anyone; everything has its price.'

She was utterly shocked at the bald statement and her face reflected this, but the sapphire eyes were cool and unconcerned as they gazed back at her.

'That's not true.' She knew that she wouldn't even make a mark on that tough hide of his but she just couldn't let such a remark go by without challenging it. 'I know there *are* people who would sell their soul, but there are plenty more who wouldn't, who live their lives without compromising their own personal standards.'

He looked hard into her troubled eyes, her flushed face and indignant voice bringing a mocking smile to his clean sculpted mouth. 'What a baby you are,' he murmured softly. 'Either that or you walk round with your eyes shut most of the time.'

The cool ridicule caught her on the raw. 'I am neither blind nor a baby,' she snapped back tightly, 'and I'm perfectly entitled to have a different opinion to you without you trying to make me feel a fool. You aren't always right, you know.'

His eyes were midnight-blue now, and unblinking, and he wasn't smiling any longer. Sephy remembered too late that no one—no one—argued with Conrad Quentin and got away with it, especially not such a lowly creature as a secretary. She swallowed deeply and waited for the explosion.

'So you're not a baby,' he said silkily, after a silence

that seemed endless. 'You are a fully grown woman with a mind of her own.'

Sephy opened her mouth to agree and then closed it again. From the look on his face this wasn't a good time for further sparring. She watched him warily as he walked across to stand in front of her, her honey-brown eyes opening wide as he stretched out one strong hand and pulled her to her feet.

The top of her head just reached his big, broad shoulders and every cell in her body was reacting to his dangerous proximity as his powerfully muscled chest beneath the thin silk of his shirt came frighteningly close. He kept his hold on her fragile wrist with one hand, his other snaking round her waist and pulling her in to him so the scent and warmth of him was all about her.

'You have the air of an ingenue,' he murmured, as she raised her face to look at him, 'and you're as scented and soft as any true innocent. But by your own admission you are an independent career girl with her sights set on the top of the ladder, so you can't be all you seem, can you? It takes a tough cookie to survive in this arena we call the business world. Do you think you've got what it takes, Sephy, to fight your way to the summit?'

The hand which had been holding her wrist slid under her small chin as he forced her head further back so he could look deep into her eyes and his voice was uncompromisingly grim.

Sephy wanted to wrench herself out of his grasp and verbally floor him with a cuttingly cold put-down, but for the life of her she couldn't move or speak. The magnetic quality of his dark attractiveness was enhanced tenfold, a hundredfold, by his nearness. He had loosened his tie at some point during their conversation and also undone a couple of the top buttons of his shirt—a habit of his, she now acknowledged—and consequently, with the tie askew, she could see silky dark hairs below his collarbone.

Was he hairy all over? It was a ridiculously inappropriate thought in the circumstances, but she found she couldn't concentrate on anything but what his body was doing to hers by its closeness.

'No, you're not what you seem,' he said contemplatively, as though he was thinking out loud. 'Take your hair; I thought it was dark brown at first, but there are myriad colours in it when the light catches it and it turns to spun silk.' The hand left her small chin to wander into the nape of her neck where his fingers stroked her soft skin thoughtfully. 'And your eyes, liquid gold...'

She was standing perfectly still now, frozen in his light grasp and not daring to breathe as his husky voice continued, 'And then there's those freckles. What hard-bitten career woman has freckles these days, for goodness' sake? Freckles belong on young, carefree children, playing in the sun through long summer days when the corn is high and the nights are endless.'

'I...' She had to move, to say something to break the spell he was casting over her. 'My mother has freckles.'

'Ah, yes, the redhead.' He nodded as the slanted blue gaze locked with soft gold. 'And that would explain the colours in your hair; you're a redhead under that façade of prim brunette.' He made it sound wicked, indecent even, as though he had discovered she was wearing titillating erotic underwear in an effort to seduce him, and she found herself blushing scarlet.

'And this.' He touched her burning cheeks with a light, mocking finger. 'I thought it'd gone out of fashion years ago, along with men giving up their seats on buses for the weaker sex and protecting the fair lady of their choice by walking on the outside.' He smiled lazily, his eyes narrowing still more as the tip of her red tongue appeared, to moisten lips that were suddenly dry. 'And then you had to come along,' he added softly. 'My stern little secretary.'

'Your stern little *temporary* secretary,' she corrected shakily, knowing she had to defuse the tensely vibrating atmosphere before— Before what? she asked herself silently. Before he kissed her? But he wouldn't do that, not Conrad Quentin. Would he?

She was gazing at him, mesmerised, and she was sure the dark tanned face was coming nearer, the piercing blue of his eyes holding hers with a power that was unbreakable, and then...

'The dinner, it is ready!' Daniella's voice called out just a second before the beautiful Italian opened the drawing room door. But, although Sephy jerked in his hold, and pushed away from him, hotly embarrassed, Conrad's hold tightened for a moment or two before he let her go—certainly long enough for Daniella to be aware of their position.

'Shall we?'

He was every inch the cool suave host and charming dinner companion as he gestured for Sephy to follow Daniella to the dining room, and as Sephy glanced at the other woman she saw nothing but a sweet smile on her face. Nevertheless, she had never felt so acutely uncomfortable in her life as she walked out of the room, and she vowed, with every step, that at some point in the next hour or so she would find some way of telling Conrad Quentin that the arrangement was off. She was returning to the innocuous sanctuary of Customer Services forthwith, and if he didn't like it— Well, she'd cross that bridge when she came to it!

The bitter experience of her youth had taught her that some people were quite capable of playing cruel and dangerous games with no thought of anyone else but themselves, and she rather thought Conrad Quentin fell into that category.

He was the sort of man who would totally dominate any relationship he embarked on; everything about him proclaimed it. There would be no sharing with him, no compromise, no meeting point, and she just didn't want to be around someone like that.

Of course he hadn't been about to kiss her, she reassured herself silently. That had been her wild imagination, that was all. He did that—made her think crazy thoughts—and she didn't know why. Which was another good reason for not working for him.

But he was a womaniser. That *wasn't* her imagination. And a dyed-in-the-wool bachelor with a woman for every day of the week and even one at home!

But if he thought he might be getting one at the office too he could think again!

CHAPTER FOUR

AS IT happened the chance to tell Conrad she wanted to return to Mr Harper came and went a few times during the excellent meal which Daniella served them, but every time Sephy opened her mouth to grasp it she lost her nerve.

This was partly due to the perturbation she was feeling as she sat opposite Conrad at the magnificent dining table in a room that matched the drawing room for opulence. But the fact that Daniella was forever popping in and out, and also that Conrad had metamorphosed into engaging, butter-wouldn't-melt-in-his-mouth host, didn't help either.

However, once she had spooned the last remnants of a quite wonderful lemon soufflé into her mouth, and a smiling Daniella had taken their order for coffee, Sephy steeled herself for the inevitable. She would be short and concise and firm, she told herself silently, and she wouldn't be persuaded to deviate from her decision, even if he threatened her with dismissal. She couldn't handle this—she couldn't handle *him*—it was another world from the one she was used to. If this was what was entailed in being the secretary to a high-flying tycoon she'd settle for dumpy little Mr Harper any day.

'Mr Quentin—'

Black brows frowned at her and she hastily qualified, 'Conrad. I need to say something.'

'Fire away.' He settled back more easily into the large antique carving chair and she forced her eyes not to flinch from the searching scrutiny of the laser-sharp gaze. She couldn't afford to show any weakness in front of this man—she already knew him well enough to know that!

There had been a telephone ringing somewhere in the house a few moments before, and now, as Sephy opened her mouth to speak, there was a tap at the dining room door which was the prelude to Daniella entering a second later.

'It is Mr Walton,' she said quickly. 'He say it very important he speak with you. He sound upset, very upset.'

'Walton?' Conrad's brow wrinkled as Daniella handed him the telephone, and he glanced at Sephy, saying briefly, 'Excuse me a moment, would you? Walton's the manager of a company I've set up recently in the States and there's been a few teething troubles which I thought were sorted,' before he spoke a few succinct words into the receiver.

There was silence for a moment or two, and from Conrad's darkening face Sephy assumed the news was not good. The jovial, charming, amusing dinner companion had vanished, and in his place was the cold hard man who was a legend in his own lifetime in business circles.

'Don't do anything until I get there.' It was a terse bark, and Sephy inwardly flinched for the hapless Mr Walton. Then, as the phone was slammed down with a great deal more force than was necessary and he raised his head, she stiffened. 'It looks like I'm on the next plane,' he said mildly, with a complete change of tone as he looked straight at Daniella. 'Arrange it, would you? There should be something later tonight or early morning. I need to get out there and see what's going on for myself.'

'Tonight?' It was Sephy who squeaked the word, and now the diamond-hard eyes focused on her, but she could see he was already concentrating on the problem in the States and was only with her in body. He had gone into work mode.

'You'll hold the fort.' It was a statement not a question. 'You've work for a couple of days, haven't you?'

Sephy nodded dazedly.

'And I'll fax any instructions, as well as communicating

by phone, of course. You've got Madge's keys now, so you have access to everything you need.'

She nodded again; it was all she could manage. She had heard of living life in the fast lane but Conrad's lifestyle was something else. Grand Prix speed.

'Could you ask Enrico to take Sephy home, Daniella, before you make that phone call?' he asked smoothly, and then, as the housekeeper scurried from the room, he smiled at Sephy and said softly, 'I'm sorry for such an abrupt ending to our meal.'

'Who's Enrico?' she asked bewildered. She had thought he and Daniella lived here alone.

And then, in the instant the smile became shark-like, she realised he had known what she had been thinking all along. 'Enrico is Daniella's husband,' he said easily as his lids dropped lazily, hiding his expression for a moment. 'He is training to be a chef and had the chance to work in a big London restaurant, so it seemed opportune for the pair of them to live with me for a time. Daniella insists on looking after things, which isn't necessary, of course. She is my niece after all.' And the lids raised as mocking blue eyes took in her confusion with a relish that wasn't lost on Sephy.

His niece! He had known what she was thinking and all the time he had been playing a game with her. But if Daniella was his niece that meant she was his dead sister's child.

As if in answer to her thoughts, he said silkily, 'When Janette left England she ran away with her lover, Daniella's Italian father, and they married once they were in Italy. When Daniella was born some years later her birth prompted my sister to seek out my parents, to see if some sort of relationship could possibly be established. She wasn't sure of her reception and so they decided—her husband and herself—that she would come alone. That decision probably saved the lives of Daniella's father and Daniella, but meant my niece had only one parent to bring her up. And a host of Italian relatives, of course,' he added with a wry smile.

Sephy took a much-needed gulp of the last of her wine, draining the glass before she said, 'So you do have some family you're close to?'

'Close to?' He considered the words as he rose from his chair, his big masculine body moving with surprisingly lithe grace as he walked over to the window and stood with his back to her, staring out into the dark vista beyond the lighted room.

He said nothing for a moment or two, and then he turned, his eyes hooded and distant as he said, 'I don't think I'm capable of being close to anyone, Sephy. I simply don't know how. The Jesuits used to say, "Give us a child until he is seven and we'll have him for life", and I can agree with the philosophy. I lived a solitary existence as a child before I was packed off to boarding school when I was seven years old, like my sister before me, and frankly I wouldn't be where I am now if that had been different, so perhaps it was a blessing in disguise.'

'No.' The word left her lips without her volition, brought up from the very depths of her being. 'You can't really believe that,' she protested painfully. 'Not deep inside.'

'Why?' he asked coolly. 'Why should that be so difficult to accept? Because it happens to be different to what you believe?'

'No, no, it's not that. It's just…' Her voice trailed away as she searched for words to make him *see*. 'You're missing out on so much if you don't ever let yourself fall in love and be loved,' she said earnestly. And then she stopped, shocked to the core at what she had said. Here she was preaching at Conrad and what had she been doing for the last eight years? she asked herself silently. Talk about the pot calling the kettle black!

'Missing out?' he echoed mockingly, a cutting edge to the sarcasm. 'Missing out on betrayal, heartache, divorce, alimony payments? Because that's what inevitably happens once this myth called love—which is nothing more than natural animal attraction, incidentally—fades and dies. Or perhaps I'm missing out on staying with someone who drives me mad, and who I, in turn, probably drive mad, for the sake of offspring who eventually will go off and live their own lives and not care a jot about me? Believe me, Sephy, if that's what I'm missing out on it suits me just fine.'

Sephy did not know how to answer, but she was appalled at the cynicism he had revealed, and Conrad, perhaps sensing this, smiled indulgently as he walked over to her and lifted her shocked, tragic face up to meet his eyes. 'Such a baby,' he murmured very softly, and then, as he continued staring into the drowning, liquid gold of her thickly lashed eyes his expression changed.

His head lowered, his probing lips taking her tremulous, soft mouth in a kiss that was meant to be light and teasing but which swiftly turned into something fiery the second their mouths touched, something incredibly sweet and wild.

Dimly Sephy realised she was kissing him back, but, locked in his arms as she was, with the smell and feel of this big harsh magnetic man all about her, all coherent thought seemed to have fled. For another second the kiss deepened, and then Conrad made a low guttural sound of protest, lifting his head and letting go of her as he stepped back a pace.

It was him who had stopped. It was *him*. That was the one and only thought in her head initially as she faced him, her colour coming and going in a face that was chalk-white.

And then he sighed heavily, his eyes raking her face as

he said softly, 'Don't look like that, Sephy. In spite of all the signs to the contrary I'm not about to leap on you and ravish you on the carpet, and please believe me when I say I have never taken advantage of my position to act in such a way before.'

He made a movement to put out his hand to her, but when she flinched he withdrew it immediately, his mouth tightening.

Why had he kissed her? She stared at him as she desperately tried to pull herself together. She believed him when he said he didn't make a habit of seducing his employees. In fact it was a well-known fact that he had never so much as given any of the girls a Christmas kiss, in spite of the way some of the more confident of his female employees had thrown themselves at him.

And then he seemed to answer the question himself, making her even more ashamed and humiliated by her reaction to his lips when he said, 'You just looked so...lost for a moment. Hell!' He raked back a lock of black hair from his forehead with an impatient hand. 'That's no excuse; I know that.'

'It...it's all right.' She had transferred her gaze to somewhere just over his left shoulder and it helped. He was too dark and dangerous, too attractive, with his shirt half undone and his hair ruffled, for her to be able to speak and look at him at the same time. *Lost*. He had thought she looked lost. It was the final blow to her fragile self-esteem. He hadn't been prompted by desire or even the tiniest shot of lust—he had felt sorry for her. And what had she done? Practically eaten him! After all she'd said about rarely dating and so on, he'd think she was sex-starved.

The thought caused her face to become brilliant, but it put steel in her backbone and enabled her to draw herself up straight and say, with a composure that was born purely of fierce pride, 'It really is all right. Let's forget it, shall we? It's late and it's been an exhausting day. Please, you go and do whatever you need to do to get ready to leave for the airport. I'll wait for Enrico here.'

As though on cue, Daniella tapped on the dining room door in the next instant, this time entering with a small, plump, slightly balding man who was the very antithesis of the stunningly beautiful Italian woman, but whose smile was sweet and manner gentle as he introduced himself.

Sephy was aware she was working on automatic as she smiled and conversed with Conrad and the others in the minute or so before she left the room, but then, thankfully, she was outside in the cool mellow air.

Once ensconced in the car, she raised a brief hand of farewell to Conrad and Daniella, who were standing in the lighted doorway, and then sank back limply against the seat once the powerful car had nosed its way out of the drive. She listened to Enrico enthusing about England, his work, and how *grateful* he and Daniella had been when Conrad had offered them a home once they had decided to come to England. By the time they reached Islington her nerves were stretched to breaking point.

The night was throbbing with the sounds of Maisie's party, but she managed to reach the flat and fall into the hall without anyone seeing her. She leant against the front door for some long minutes, her eyes tightly shut and her face beginning to burn again as she let herself relive those few moments in Conrad's arms, and then she walked through to the bathroom and ran herself a steaming hot bath.

She lay in the bubbly scented water until it was cool and she cried on and off the whole time, but when, eventually, she padded through to the bedroom to dry her hair she felt better for the release of emotion. It was a kiss, that was all it had been, and nothing to get upset about, she reassured herself for the umpteenth time. In this day and age a kiss meant absolutely nothing! He wasn't remotely attracted to her and that was fine—a hundred per cent fine; she couldn't have remained working for him if he was. Not someone like Conrad Quentin.

His image on the screen of her mind brought her heart thumping and her stomach churning again, and she shook herself irritably, angry at her reaction. Okay, so he was an attractive and charismatic kind of guy, with the added bonus of power and wealth and goodness knows what; it wasn't at all surprising she'd been knocked off guard tonight, she concluded firmly. That was how she had to look at this.

She reiterated the thought over and over again, and then walked through to the small fitted kitchen where she made herself a strong cup of black coffee.

Conrad Quentin had every aphrodisiac in the book going for him, and she was only human; in fact she should perhaps consider it a blessing that she could feel the way she had when he kissed her after all the years of fancying no one. She'd thought more than once that David had made her frigid, and if nothing else that theory had been well and truly smashed!

He had made it abundantly plain he had no intention of repeating the exercise—she didn't like the little twinge her heart gave at this point and hastily went on—and so she could work the few weeks before Madge returned secure in the knowledge that it couldn't do her career any harm at all. There was no problem, there really wasn't, and she mustn't create one.

And the way he had been before dinner? a little voice in her head questioned. He had held her then, and said her hair was like spun silk and her eyes liquid gold...

Enough. It was harsh and final. He hadn't meant anything by it—his reaction to her when she had kissed him back had proved that—and she had been gauche and naive to panic and want to scuttle back to the safety of Mr Harper and Customer Services like a frightened rabbit.

Thank goodness she hadn't said anything during the meal about returning to her old job. She breathed in the rich fragrance of coffee beans as her eyes narrowed. He would have thought she was mad! She couldn't have given any logical reason for such a decision. *No, she could do this.* She could work for Conrad Quentin until Madge was better; she owed herself this chance to prove she was up there with the best of them.

She nodded at the thought, picked up the coffee mug and went to bed.

The next few days proved to be an anticlimax.

The emergency in the States developed into more of a crisis than Conrad had first expected, and apart from one or two terse phone calls—one of which requested that Sephy visit Madge at the hospital with reassurances as to Angus's welfare—he didn't contact the England office.

Sephy had finished the work he had given her by the second day, and the third morning found her in the unusual position of searching out things to do. It was a useful breathing space in which to familiarise herself with current files, procedures, problems and the like, and the couple of visits she'd made to the hospital helped in that regard too.

Madge seemed to have taken a liking to her, and, far from being defensive and wary—as Sephy had half expected the elderly spinster might be in view of her fierce hold on both her boss and her job—she had proved to be a mine of information about matters great and small. Sephy discovered a wicked sense of humour under the austere outer shell, and also a wry, slightly cynical way of looking at things that helped Sephy to understand why Madge's partnership with her young, dynamic boss was such a successful one. They were really very much alike.

The weekend was taken up with painting the flat's sitting room. When Sephy had moved into her new dwelling place some weeks before she had loved the decor, apart from this particular room which had been a dingy shade of green. By the time Monday morning dawned she was eating her breakfast at the little table by the sitting room window surrounded by sunshine-yellow, her new curtains of warm ochre cotton and carpet of a pale buttery hue toning in perfectly, causing her to glance round several times in satisfied perusal of her hard work.

The flat was costing an arm and a leg, and she wouldn't be able to afford anything more than paint after the extravagance of the new curtains and carpet for months and months, but it was worth it. Situated above the shops as they were, the row of flats looked out over rooftops and a wide expanse of light-washed sky, and after years of managing in a tiny rundown bedsit Sephy felt she had come home.

Life was good and it was going to get better. That was in the nature of a declaration, and she wasn't quite sure why she had to emphasise it in her mind, but later, as she walked into her office and saw the interconnecting door open and Conrad already seated at his desk, she repeated the silent vow.

'Good morning.' He glanced up briefly from the papers on his desk, the vivid sapphire gaze taking in her upswept hair and the smart dusky-red suit she was wearing before returning to the open file in front of him.

'Good morning.' The all-encompassing glance had thrown her slightly, but her voice was cool and steady even as her face turned the same shade as her suit.

'Order us some coffee, would you? And then bring in your notebook and pen. It's going to be a busy morning.' His voice was preoccupied and he didn't look up again.

It set the tone for the next few weeks.

Conrad was an exacting employer, who expected his secretary to work long into the night when circumstances demanded it. He never tired—at least Sephy never saw any signs of it—and his mind was as razor-sharp at the end of a gruelling day as first thing in the morning.

Even on the days she left the offices at roughly the normal time she was too exhausted to do more than fix herself a quick sandwich at home before falling into bed, and the weekends were simply rounds of sleep, and more sleep, with the week's washing being squeezed in somewhere along with a quick clean of the flat.

But even before she received her first pay-cheque in the role of Conrad's temporary secretary—which was treble the amount she received in Customer Services and made her sit down very suddenly as she stared in disbelief at the row of figures—she relished the job. It was exciting and stimulating and she couldn't wait to get to work in the morning.

All the years of covering for Mr Harper had stood her in good stead—she thrived on challenge and wasn't afraid of responsibility or using her own initiative; all essential in her role as Madge's replacement.

Conrad never once alluded to the night he had taken her to his home—he probably had never thought of it again, she told herself drily. Instead he simply used her as his right-hand man—more of a personal assistant than a secretary—and was always perfectly correct and businesslike, to the point where she couldn't remember him so much as touching her. When he looked at her he probably saw a small compact computer on legs! Which was perfect, ideal, *splendid*! It was; it *really* was, she told herself when she wasn't too tired to think. She was another Madge Watkins to him, which was…splendid.

On the sixth weekend her mother arrived unexpectedly on her doorstep, worried by the amount of times she had phoned an empty flat, only to learn later Sephy had been working late. The two of them spent a day sightseeing and acting like tourists, before staying up half the night drinking cheap red wine and talking about everything under the sun. Everything except Conrad Quentin. For some reason—and Sephy couldn't explain it, even to herself—she couldn't bring herself to discuss her boss.

And it was on the Monday morning following her mother's visit that it happened.

The day had begun like every other working day over the last six weeks except that—the November morning being a stormy one, with dark skies and heavy rain—she had accepted the offer of a lift to work from Jerry, who was on his way to see his solicitor in Woolwich. They had collided on the doorstep just as Sephy was leaving for work, umbrella in hand, and she had been grateful to slide into Jerry's old but very presentable BMW.

The ten-minute walk took just as long by car in the rush hour, but at least she was in the dry and travelling in comfort. She hadn't seen anything of Jerry—she hadn't seen anything of anybody!—since she had been standing in for Madge, although she had slipped along to Maisie the first weekend after the party and explained her new position. And it was Jerry, his manner somewhat diffident, who broached the matter of her absence from the social get-togethers.

'There's a bunch of us going to the theatre next week, but I suppose you won't be able to make it with the new job and all?' he said quietly, the windscreen wipers swishing frantically at the torrential flow.

Sephy hesitated. If she was being absolutely truthful she probably could—there had been several occasions over the last weeks when she could have joined in what the others were doing, especially at the weekends, but the job had been an opportune excuse to distance herself from Jerry's affections. And she *had* been exhausted most nights, she told herself firmly to assuage the pang of guilt. 'I might,' she said carefully, 'but there's always the chance of some crisis or other.'

'The thing is, Sephy...' His voice trailed away and she was aware of him taking a deep breath before he went on, his voice resolute, 'I need to ask you something.'

'Yes?' She prayed he wasn't going to ask her out again.

'I think I know the answer, you've made it pretty clear in the nicest way possible of course, but...' The car had just reached the top of the road wherein Quentin Dynamics was situated, and Jerry negotiated the BMW past parked cars on either side before nipping into a parking space right outside the front doors of the building. 'Is there any hope at all for me?' he asked with sudden and surprising directness as he cut the engine and turned in his seat to face her. 'With you, I mean?'

She had been expecting something of the sort, but it didn't stop the flood of colour washing over her face as she stared back into his nice, good-looking face. 'Jerry, I like you, very much, as a friend,' she managed unevenly, wishing she was more adept at this sort of thing. 'But as anything more... No. I'm sorry.'

'It's all right.' He smiled at her, his puppy-dog eyes as friendly as ever, which made Sephy feel worse. 'I needed to know, that's all. You see, Maisie and I are hitting it off rather well, but I had to make sure with you first. But if there's no chance...' He shrugged and she saw he was keeping the smile in place with some effort. 'I've nothing to lose, have I? And Maisie is a lovely girl. She's had a rough deal in life, actually, rotten childhood by all accounts, and behind all the hair and rings and things she's quite insecure and sensitive.'

Jerry and *Maisie*? The easy-going, public school, correct Englishman and the outlandish, wild, flamboyant Maisie? But why not? Sephy thought in the next instant. Opposites attract, and there *was* something very vulnerable about Maisie when she thought about it. Yes, she could see it working. He would look after Maisie, and she would bring out the fun-loving side of Jerry that was lurking under the surface. They were two very intelligent, ambitious individuals with more in common than was apparent at first. Yes, it could be a terrific partnership, given the chance.

'I think you and Maisie are perfect for each other,' Sephy said warmly, 'I really do. She needs someone like you, Jerry, a *real* person and a gentleman to boot.'

'Thank you.' And now his smile wasn't strained any more as he said, 'Can I kiss you, as a friend?'

'Sure.' She smiled at him, her eyes warm.

She leant forward and their lips touched briefly as he hugged her tight for one moment before they settled back in their seats, and Jerry was just saying, a touch of laughter in his voice, 'And you can be bridesmaid, eh?' when there was a sharp tap on the passenger window, which nearly caused Sephy to jump into Jerry's lap in fright.

Conrad Quentin was glaring at them—that was the only word she could use, Sephy thought with a touch of silent hysteria—as she surveyed the cold, harsh face of her boss through the glass.

'What the...?'

As Jerry began to speak, his tone the angriest she had ever heard it, Sephy put one hand over his and said quickly, 'It's all right, really, Jerry, I'll sort it. Thanks for the lift, but just go now, would you?'

'Are you sure?' he asked doubtfully, and then, as Conrad had the audacity to smack on the glass again, with enough power to make it shake, Sephy saw Jerry's face change and quickly opened the car door. She had heard it said the quietest ones were the worst when they got going, and Jerry looked as though he was about to do murder.

'I'll see you tonight,' she said hurriedly, before she

slammed the door shut and walked straight past the tall, dark figure at the side of the car, intent only on keeping the two men apart.

She was already in the foyer of the building when Conrad caught up with her, and she could see he was furious with the type of white-hot rage that could explode at any moment. Nevertheless, he didn't say a word as he joined her in the lift, and neither did she, and it was like that that they travelled up to the top floor and entered the outer office.

But before the door had even had time to close, Sephy had whirled to face him. 'How dare you? How *dare* you behave like that?' she said furiously as their eyes locked. She hadn't lost her temper in years, but suddenly all her mother's spirited red-headed genes took over with a vengeance, and although she knew—somewhere in the depths of her—that it was goodbye to her job, to the nice fat salary that paid the bills, no power on earth could have stopped her.

'How dare *I*?' he ground out, anger making the blue of his eyes steely. He was wearing a heavy black overcoat, which increased the overall impression of dark strength and power, and the moments in the rain had caused his short black hair, a lock of which had fallen across his tanned forehead, to curl slightly. It was the only hint of softness in an otherwise formidable countenance. 'You expect me to allow my secretary to sit necking in full view of the rest of the staff?' he bit out savagely.

'Necking?' She ignored the tense set of his jaw and the splintered bolts of blue shooting from his eyes. 'I wasn't necking! I exchanged a peck of a kiss, nothing more, and I don't have to explain to you anyway,' she added vehemently. 'I work for you, that's all, and as it's only—' she consulted the pretty lacy wristwatch that had been a twenty-first birthday present from her mother '—twenty to nine, I'm not even officially doing that at the moment.'

'Wrong.' He eyed her grimly, his mouth taut. 'As my personal secretary there are certain standards you adhere to at all times.'

Standards? He dared to lecture her about standards— moral standards—when he had had more women than she'd had hot dinners? she thought venomously. He had been waiting for her to slip from grace in some way; she just knew it! She had caught him, several times over the last weeks, surveying her coldly from icy-blue eyes as though she was a bug under a microscope.

She didn't measure up to his precious Madge, obviously, but the covert scrutiny had only had the effect of making her work her socks off to prove herself, so he had nothing to grumble about. If nothing else she had given value for money and he knew it! He knew it all right.

Sephy drew herself up to her full five feet six inches and took a deep breath before she said, her voice withering, 'Then perhaps it's better if I resign as your secretary?'

'Taking the easy way out?'

The easy way out! The contempt in his voice caused her to want to do or say something to hurt him, really hurt him, and it shocked her to the core. She had never in all her life wanted to harm another human being, not even David, and now here she was, in real danger of losing control. The thought checked her, enabling her to say tightly, 'I won't be spoken to like that, Mr Quentin.'

'If you're trying to make this worse with the ''Mr Quentin'' tactic then you are succeeding,' he snapped harshly.

How had she ever got herself into this position? The thought was there in the midst of the awfulness of the moment. Six or seven weeks ago she had been jogging along quite happily, secure in the knowledge she had found the home of her dreams, which she could—just—pay for, and that her life at work and home was tranquil. Admittedly there had been Jerry to deal with, but in comparison to Conrad... Well, there was no comparison.

Conrad Quentin seemed to think he could ride roughshod over all and sundry and get away with it—mainly because he did! But enough was enough. He might be heart-thumpingly attractive, with that certain undefinable something, but she was determined to show him how wrong he had been to jump to such an erroneous conclusion regarding Jerry. Then, having explained, she would walk out of here with some dignity, if nothing else.

'I'm not trying to make anything worse,' she snapped back sharply now, 'but you are the most provoking—' She stopped abruptly. 'I've worked for you until I've dropped over the last few weeks,' she continued stiffly, after one swift glance at his rigidly cold face that was granite-hard, 'and I am the last person in the world to take the easy way out. If I'd been going to do that I'd have left the day after I started working for you.' You impossible man, she added silently.

'I'm not questioning your efficiency at work, or your aptitude,' he stated harshly, and then, as he raked back the errant lock of hair from his forehead—something he was apt to do when he was disturbed, she'd noticed in the last weeks—Sephy had the most alarming desire to burst into tears.

She clenched her teeth against the weakness, refusing to acknowledge the trembling in her limbs the confrontation had produced, and prayed for enough composure to be able to say what was needed before she walked out. 'I thought I had made it plain weeks ago that Jerry and I are just friends,' she said tightly. 'He gave me a lift to work because of the rain, that's all, and he'd just told me he was

seeing someone else, as it happens. I…I congratulated him
and we exchanged a friendly hug.'

'A friendly hug.' It was expressionless, but nevertheless
it had the effect of catching her on the raw. 'And the kiss?
Was that friendly too?'

'I don't lie, Conrad.' It was the last straw, the very last
straw. The colour had flooded back into her face and her
eyes glittered with outrage. 'And I don't appreciate being
made to look ridiculous in front of my friends either. Your
behaviour, not mine, was outrageous, but, like I said, you
can have my resignation right now.'

'In the six weeks since we've been working together you
have resigned twice, once on the first day,' he said evenly,
after a long pause when Sephy continued to stare back at
him, refusing to drop her eyes or in any way appear deferential. 'What do you suppose that suggests?'

'I've no idea.' His tone was suddenly too smooth and
she didn't trust him. He was looking at her in that strange
way again, which caused further flutters in her stomach.
'But if I had to take a guess I'd say it might be that it
shows you'd have been better off with Marilyn or Philippa
or one of the other secretaries?'

'Marilyn or Philippa?' The names were said with deep
disgust as his eyes narrowed into laser keenness. 'I think
not. You suit me, Sephy. You suit me very well.'

His tack *had* changed. She swallowed hard, finding herself suddenly at a loss. She had seen it before—this mer-
curial ability to totally change direction in the midst of a
heated discussion. He used the ploy often in business, usually with devastating consequences to his opponents, leaving them confused at best and at his mercy at worst. But
she was *not* confused, she reassured herself silently, and
neither was she at Conrad Quentin's mercy!

'Would it be very crass of me to say it wouldn't appear
so from this morning's episode?' she asked doggedly with

flat directness, calling on all her resources and looking him in the eye.

'No, not crass, merely misguided,' he answered smilingly, good humour apparently perfectly restored. 'I'm never bored with you, Sephy, and that's quite a compliment if you did but know it. I bore easily. Madge never bores me either,' he added softly.

'Oh, good.' It was deeply sarcastic, and she wasn't quite sure why she felt so affronted, but the urge to knock the satisfied arrogant smile from his dark face was strong. 'I'm glad Madge and I have our uses,' she said scathingly.

He gave a soft laugh and she could tell he was really genuinely amused. That made her madder.

'No man in his right mind would compare some of your uses with Madge's,' he said silkily, his eyes taking on a smoky hue as they wandered over the thick silk of her hair for a moment. 'And Madge has certainly never been responsible for challenging one concept I have always held dear.'

'Which is?' She hadn't really wanted to ask but she needed to know the answer.

'Never to mix business with pleasure,' he answered smoothly, before turning and walking into his office and shutting the door.

CHAPTER FIVE

THE two months until Madge returned to work were difficult ones for Sephy. Not that Conrad was anything less than the perfect boss—polite, detached, fair and supportive—but all the time she was on edge.

It was as though the incident on the morning Jerry had given her a lift to work had opened a Pandora's box of emotions, and she could never quite get the lid on it again.

She went over and over his last words to her on that caustic occasion until she thought she'd go mad, and finally came to the conclusion that he *couldn't* have meant what she had—foolishly—thought he was suggesting. He didn't seriously fancy her; she would know if he did, she told herself firmly, several days after the episode had happened. He had merely been giving her a brief, placatory compliment because he had known—even before she did—she'd taken umbrage at being viewed in the same way as the elderly spinster.

No, he didn't *fancy* her—the comment had been a sop to her feminine pride, that was all, she finally decided, and as his cool attitude confirmed the conclusion without any shadow of a doubt that should have been the end of the matter. But somehow, since that fateful day, all her senses seemed to be tuned to breaking point if he was anywhere in the vicinity, and he ruthlessly invaded her head every night with such erotic dreams that she blushed to think about them in the cold harsh light of morning.

As the Christmas party approached she secretly degenerated into a bag of nerves whilst telling herself that whereas everyone else might let their hair down and flirt outrageously Conrad had never been known to as much as dabble in a spot of chatting up. And then, two days before Christmas Eve, twenty-four hours before the party, he called her very early to tell her he was leaving within the hour for Germany, to finalise a deal they had been setting up for weeks with a leading electronics firm who had finally—and very suddenly—capitulated to Conrad's terms.

And that was that. She went into work later that morning to find a Christmas card, with a mind-blowingly generous Christmas box in the form of a cheque tucked inside, on her desk. The card read, 'Have a great Christmas, Sephy, and please accept the cheque with many thanks for helping out. C.'

'C'. She stared at the scrawled initial for some time. He hadn't even bothered to write his name. And 'helping out' couldn't have made it plainer she was a very transitory figure in his life. Which she had known all the time, of course. *Of course*. She was a sensible, mature woman, wasn't she?

She hired a car and drove to Banbury to spend Christmas with her mother, and the two of them indulged in a truly traditional Christmas Eve by decorating the little cottage and trimming the tree as they drank hot mulled wine and ate too many mince-pies.

They woke up to snow on Christmas Day—great white flakes that settled immediately and turned the village into a chocolate-box wonderland—and after a service in the thirteenth-century parish church trudged home to a roaring log fire, turkey and plum pudding, followed by the Queen's speech.

Friends from the hospital where her mother worked called round for tea in the afternoon and stayed all evening, and they were invited out on Boxing Day to a party at one of the consultants' homes, which went on into the early hours.

The holiday flew by in a festive haze of eating, drinking and making merry, and Sephy enjoyed herself—she really did—so why was it, she asked herself during the drive back to London, that all the time a tall, dark, blue-eyed spectre had been broodingly present on the edge of her consciousness?

And then the New Year swept in, at one of Maisie's wildly sensational parties; a wet, damp spell removed the last trace of the holiday spirit, and the first three weeks of January were gone in a hectic spell at the office which had her working twelve- and fourteen-hour days and even through all one weekend.

So she ought to have been glad—delighted, even—when, on the last Monday in January, Conrad stopped by her desk on the way into his office and said, his voice crisp and businesslike, 'Good news by the way, Sephy. Madge has had the all-clear and is returning to work next week. I've said you'll take the day off on Friday and spend it at her home, acquainting her with anything you think is important and bringing her up to date on the bigger events of the last three months.'

They looked at each other for a second, her honey-brown eyes wide with shock and his crystal-clear blue gaze as cold and deep as an arctic sea. Good news. She was going and it was good news?

'Yes, yes, of course.' His utter detachment enabled her to draw on her pride and answer as coolly as he had spoken. 'I'll clear out my things on Thursday afternoon.'

For a second his eyes narrowed, a flare of something she couldn't understand at the back of them. Then the hard male head nodded abruptly and he passed her without another word, although she thought his door was shut on something of a bang before she assured herself she must be mistaken.

Just like that! No thank you, no word of appreciation,

she thought grimly. The man was a machine, a mass of steel components made into the likeness of a human being. She had never known anyone who could keep themselves so aloof on a personal level as Conrad. And yet the evening of that first day she had worked for him— She caught hold of the thought sternly. She had made a vow to herself to put that out of her mind and she'd succeeded...most of the time.

It didn't matter that the long days she had worked for Conrad, often until well into the night when all the other staff had gone home, leaving just the two of them in their luxurious eyrie high at the top of the building, had meant she had got to know every little mannerism and characteristic of this powerful, magnetic man. She knew what the downward quirk of his firm bottom lip meant—trouble for someone! And the way he raised one black eyebrow ever so slightly just before he went in for the kill on a business deal. And...oh, hundreds of things. But just because they had virtually lived in each other's pockets for several months, that didn't mean she was any nearer to breaking into that formidable, essentially private part of him than anyone else was.

She stared at her word processor in horror. Where had that thought come from? she asked herself silently. The last thing, the very last thing she needed in her life was any sort of complication with someone like Conrad Quentin. Not that he would dream of looking at her twice, of course.

She let her mind play over the article in one of the more glossy periodicals that had surfaced recently, which had been reporting on some lavish première or other. The photograph of Conrad had been a good one, and the exquisite blonde hanging like a limpet on his arm had looked extremely pleased with herself. As well she might, Sephy thought sourly.

Sephy had derived a moment's comfort from the fact that

the woman was not Caroline de Menthe—only because she didn't think Caroline was right for him, she had assured herself immediately—but the more she had examined the blonde's face and figure the quicker the brief consolation had faded. The girl was gorgeous, truly gorgeous, and was obviously the latest string to Conrad's well-used and energetic bow.

She had just packed the last of her personal items in the small cardboard box she had brought into the office on Thursday evening when Conrad strode into the office.

He had been out all day, and as Sephy glanced up when the door opened she felt the momentary thrill that always attacked her when she wasn't fully prepared to see him. He walked across the room with a nod of acknowledgement to her quick hallo, his broad, powerful body radiating leashed strength and purpose.

She stood waiting for some command or other—he had that look about him which suggested something was afoot—but as he stopped just in front of her their glances held, and she couldn't read a thing in the steady blue gaze. It had obviously been raining outside, diamond drops of water glittered in the short black hair and his overcoat looked damp, and she found herself saying, 'I thought James had driven you in the Mercedes?' James was Conrad's chauffeur, who also was in charge of the company car park in the basement of the building.

Conrad shrugged, his fixed regard unwavering. 'He did. I got him to drop me off a couple of blocks away; I had something to collect.'

'Oh.' She lowered her lids, her thick lashes masking the confusion she was feeling. She was right, something *was* afoot, but for the life of her she couldn't work out what it was. But he was tense, even covertly excited. She sensed it.

'Sephy?' His voice was very soft and deep, and now, as she raised her eyes again, his compelling gaze held hers in a vice-like grip clothed with velvet. 'This is for you.'

She glanced at the jeweller's box in his hands—the name on the satin lid causing her eyes to open wide for a moment. It was well-known, and the sort of establishment which encouraged clients who never had to ask the price of an item into its hushed confines.

'Me?' It was a squeak and she made no effort to take the package. He hadn't really bought her something, had he?

'To say thank you for being everything I could have asked for over the last months while Madge was away,' he said, with a warm charm that made him a different man from the reserved, cold being of the last months. Dangerously different.

She stared at him, totally out of her depth, and then, as the dark face began to frown, hastily stretched out her hand with a quick, 'Thank you—thank you very much. But you really shouldn't have bought me anything. I've only been doing my job after all, and you've paid me handsomely as it is. It wasn't necessary to— Oh!' The last was a soft gasp of disbelief as she raised the lid of the box and saw the superb gold choker and matching earrings it held. The choker was made up of delicate gold stars with tiny amber stones set in exquisite detail, their beauty riveting, and the earrings were elegant and dainty in their own right. They would have cost a small fortune.

'To match your eyes,' he said softly, his tone bringing her head jerking up to meet his watchful gaze.

'I... I can't... I mean...' Her mouth had suddenly gone dry and her tongue was cleaving to the roof of her mouth. 'This is too expensive; I can't possibly accept it. You must see that?' What on earth had possessed him to do this?

'I see nothing of the sort,' he answered promptly. 'Do you like it?'

'Of course I like it. How could anyone not like it?' she said shakily. 'But that's not the point.'

'I had it specially made for you, *that's* the point.' He was eyeing her with something akin to amusement now, and his voice was still warm and possessed of something that made her skin tingle. She was seeing the man those other women saw—the beautiful women he loved and petted and cosseted—and he was sheer dynamite. And *definitely* incredibly dangerous. 'If you don't accept it I shan't give it to anyone else.'

'You could take it back to the shop,' she suggested tremblingly. He'd have to, because she wasn't accepting it.

'I could, but I wouldn't.' There was a trace of impatience colouring the smooth tones now.

'I can't accept this, I'm sorry.' Her voice was firmer now, and there was no doubt she meant what she said. 'It's very kind of you, and I do appreciate the thought, but it is far too expensive. It…it just wouldn't be right.'

It was his turn to stare at her in disbelief. He didn't say anything for a moment, merely stepping backwards a step or two until he was leaning against the interconnecting wall of the office with his arms folded over his chest and his narrowed eyes fixed on her hot face. His words confirmed his incredulous expression when he murmured, half to himself, 'You are one on your own, Seraphina Vincent, do you know that? I have never had a woman turn down such a gift before.'

And of course he would have given many women presents. It shouldn't have hurt but it did, and it panicked her, the smudge of freckles across her nose standing out in protest as hot colour came and went in her face. 'I'm sorry,' she repeated stiffly.

He cut off her voice as he said, 'And why wouldn't it

be right anyway? What does the price of a gift matter? It should be the motive behind it which counts.'

Exactly, and suddenly—though it might be terribly presumptuous on her part—she wasn't at all sure of his motives! But she couldn't say that—she was going to look the biggest fool on earth if she was wrong, and she had to be wrong. She had to. Conrad had beautiful women throwing themselves at him all the time; he wasn't going to bother with her.

'You're my boss,' she said with unintentional primness, her soft mouth trying to be stern and assertive as she called on all her wilting self-confidence.

'Not any more,' he said, with a satisfaction that started her heart thumping again. 'Why did you think I waited until today to show my appreciation?'

Help! 'You're the boss of the company anyway,' she said quickly, 'whether I work in this office or downstairs for Mr Harper.'

'True, but Customer Services is far removed enough for it not to be a problem.'

It. He wasn't talking just about the necklace and earrings. There was suddenly no doubt in Sephy's mind. *He was propositioning her.*

'You're like a drug, Sephy, one of the insidious kind that is supposed to be non-addictive,' he said softly, moving off the wall and coming to stand in front of her again, but this time at the side of her so that the desk wasn't between them. He made no attempt to touch her as he continued, 'Gentle and harmless and ordinary enough on the outside, but then, when it hits the bloodstream...'

Her utter amazement must have shown in her face, but she really couldn't believe this was the cold, controlled, autocratic figure who had been so distant over the last months. She had thought she had come to know him, just a little, but she didn't know a thing about him, she realised now. And that was scary.

She took a deep wavering breath as she fought to get a handle on the situation. Was he saying he wanted an affair with her? Was that it? A casual fling? But of course it would be that with Conrad Quentin. He had already told her on that first night in his home that he didn't go in for anything else.

She looked at him, so tall and powerful, radiating a dark virility that was more than a little exciting, and the hot little quiver that had trickled down her spine more times than she would like to admit in the last weeks made its presence known again. It was crazy, stupid—he was a carbon copy of David in all the things that mattered—but she was more attracted to this man than any other she had ever met or seen.

'What…what are you saying, exactly?' she asked at last, still nervously clutching the elegant box in her hands.

'I want you, Sephy. I want you very badly,' he said, as expressionlessly as if he was reading a train timetable. 'Is that clear enough? I would like to start seeing you—out of work.'

'Why me? You can't,' she protested shakily. 'You can't mean it.' But suddenly she had no doubt that he did.

'Why not?' he asked quietly, his eyes never leaving her face for a second. 'What's so hard to believe about it?'

'Because…' She didn't know how to put it. 'I'm not…not like Caroline de Menthe and all your other women,' she said somewhat helplessly. 'They are beautiful and glamorous and they know how to… They fit in with you,' she added weakly.

'We've done the bit about your type and mine,' he said, with a slight edge to his voice that suggested the conversation still rankled, 'and I agree with you in essence. But…'

He allowed his voice to trail away silkily as his eyes spoke their own message.

'But?' she asked when the silence became screamingly loud.

'But it doesn't explain why I still want you,' he said very softly. 'You've got under my skin in a way I can't explain, with your great golden eyes and touch-me-not façade.'

It was as if he was accusing her of something, and her voice was indignant when she said, 'It's not a façade!'

His mouth twisted. 'Two minutes—one minute—in my arms and you'd be begging me to make love to you,' he said with a raw bluntness that was challenging. 'You know it and I know it. There has been something between us from the first minute you walked into this office, and that night at my home I found myself doing something I'd never done before. Seducing one of my staff. I knew what I was doing and yet I didn't seem able to help myself, and I didn't like that, Sephy.'

Hence the ice-man from that time onwards. Suddenly it all fitted. How he would have disliked that momentary lack of control.

'When I kissed you we ignited. Admit it.' His deep voice brooked no argument. 'You wanted me as much as I wanted you but the timing was all wrong. So, I was prepared to wait.' His head tilted slightly and the sapphire gaze became piercing. 'And you've been like a cat on a hot tin roof any time I'm anywhere near you, so don't bother to deny it.'

The arrogance was overwhelming, and for a moment she was eighteen again, in the midst of a long hot summer that had turned into a living nightmare, and it was David's face stamped over Conrad's. The illusion vanished as quickly as it had come but it gave her the strength to say quietly, 'You are talking about a cheap affair, aren't you?'

'No, I am not.' He shook his head firmly. 'It wouldn't be cheap and it wouldn't be casual. I like you, Sephy, and more than that I respect you as a person. I've got to know you over the last months and I think we would be good together for as long as it lasts. How long that would be I've no idea, but it wouldn't be a brief fling. However, I can't lie to you. The things I said that night still hold.'

'You were warning me then, weren't you?' She stared at him, her brain racing. 'You were actually stating the rules of play without me realising, getting things ready for when you were prepared to make your move, and that would only be—' she took a hard deep breath as further revelation hit '—when Madge was ready to come back and you didn't need me at work any more.'

The nerve of him! The utter, absolute, cold-blooded nerve of the man! He wasn't human; he couldn't be.

'It wasn't like that,' he said quickly, but she had caught the flash of disconcertion, even astonishment, in the blue eyes, and she knew her words had hit home.

'Yes, it was,' she said with painful flatness. 'You told me that night at your home that money can buy anything and anyone, and you thought you could buy me when you considered the time was appropriate.'

No wonder he had been so angry that morning when Jerry had given her a lift to work; he had envisaged his neat programme of events being interfered with! The thought did nothing to calm her mounting rage.

'No doubt you saw me as a challenge,' she continued, as more and more things fell into place. Just as David had done all those years ago. The Ice Maiden. It had been her cruel teenage nickname that had prompted the other boys to egg David on; with Conrad it was his monstrous ego. She had dared to defy him and dispute his firmly held theories and convictions so he had to prove to her and himself that he was right. He didn't really want her; why would he, with all the stunning beauties he had at his beck and call?

'A challenge?' He considered the word for a second as she still faced him bravely, her chin lifted proudly and her eyes masking the deep hurt she was feeling. 'Yes, I guess there is an element of that in the feeling I have for you, but that's natural, isn't it? The caveman throwback, the primeval instinct to prevail and conquer in the face of adversity, to seek that which demands its worth is recognised?'

'You thought I was playing hard to get.' Her voice was tight as she placed the box on the desk with careful deliberation. 'That's it without all the soft soap. Well, I'm sorry, Conrad, but I'm not about to prostitute myself for that—' she flicked her hand at the box '—or anything else, so forget it.'

'*Prostitute yourself?*'

The charm was gone, along with the cool, faintly amused expression his face had been wearing moments before, and now Sephy felt a dart of fear as she surveyed the furiously angry man in front of her. His fists were jammed into the pockets of his overcoat as though to stop them reaching out for her neck, and his jaw was set hard, muscles working under his chiselled cheekbones. There was no doubt at all she had made her point.

'What else would you call it?' she managed faintly. A relationship on his terms was a sterile dead-end; he had *told* her that. It could never progress past the physical intimacy into true caring and loving, into wanting the best for one's partner, into tender friendship and putting another's happiness before your own. As he had said that evening months ago, he simply didn't know how. More to the point, he didn't *want* to know how. He had his empire; he had his women; his world was just as he liked it.

He glared at her, his narrowed eyes flickering with cold blue fire, and then without any warning he reached out and pulled her into his arms with enough force to jerk her head backwards. 'Perhaps we've said enough,' he rasped angrily. 'Maybe it's better if I show you.'

Sephy struggled in the instant before he bent his head and took her mouth but it was useless; she might as well be fighting the Rock of Gibraltar for all the difference it made. She was captured by his arms, his lips, his tongue; the sharp lemony flavour of his aftershave combined with the power and strength of him, reminding her of all the long days and evenings when she had been closeted in this suite of rooms fighting her awareness of him as a man.

He gave her no chance to protest, launching an experienced attack on her senses that took all logical argument clean out of her head and filled it with the magic of his closeness.

His hand cupped her head and forced her into a deeper, passionate acceptance of his lips and tongue, the exquisite sensitivity he was causing making her moan softly, low in her throat, before she could stop herself. She was dazed and shaking but enchanted, incapable of any struggle now, her body melting against him as he crushed her closer into the lean hard shape of him.

His lips scoured a hot sweet path down the line of her silky throat, causing her to quiver in response, before moving to take her mouth again as his hands roamed up and down her body, bringing shivers of delight wherever they touched.

'You can't deny this, Sephy,' he murmured huskily, 'and you know it. You want me every bit as much as I want you, and it's nothing to do with proving anything, damn it. I left that stage behind years ago.'

She sighed against his mouth, unaware that her arms had slowly drifted up to his neck, only knowing that she was melting right into him, every curve, every arch of her femininity finding its home against the virile male body pressed against hers. There was a heat in the base of her stomach that was pulsing with her heartbeat and it was intoxicating, wild, luscious.

'You taste delicious and honey-sweet,' he whispered softly as his mouth continued to plant burning kisses in between each word. 'The things I want to do to you... Hell, you can't deny us, Sephy. You know that at the heart of you. It would be so good between us. We've both known it from day one.'

She was barely aware of what he was saying; it was only his deep husky tone which was registering on the whirling light behind her closed eyelids. She felt weightless and curiously heavy at the same time with the growing ache inside her, so when the office telephone began to ring at the side of them—harsh and shrill and cutting as it bit into the bubble that surrounded her—she actually stumbled, and would have fallen but for his arms swiftly reaching out to steady her as she jerked away.

She stared wildly at him for a moment, unable to gather her scattered senses at her rude awakening from the world of colour and light his lovemaking had taken her into, and then, as she began to fumble frantically with her clothing, realising the state of her dishevelment, she saw Conrad pick up the telephone with a steady hand and speak coolly into the receiver.

He could do that! He could behave like that, when she was a melting, aching mess, she thought numbly. It was the ultimate humiliation. This hadn't affected him at all, not in his heart.

It was a moment or two before he put down the receiver and turned to look at her, and by then she was working on a feeling of outrage to cover her shame at her own complicity, at what she had allowed. 'So, that was showing me,' she stated as flatly as her pounding heart would allow. 'Do you feel better now you've got that out of your system?'

'Ah, I get it. Attack is the best defence, eh?' His voice

held a nasty edge of irony and his attitude was not reassuring.

'I'm not attacking,' she lied quickly through lips that still bore the imprint of his mouth. 'I was merely asking if your demonstration is finished. Because I would really like to go home now.'

'For crying out loud!' The words were a low growl and then she saw him breathe deeply as he mastered the brief lack of control. 'Sephy, in case you didn't know, that was no demonstration,' he mocked softly. 'I kissed you because I wanted to; I've been wanting to for months, damn it. In fact that's the least of what I want to do to you.'

'Just because you want it it doesn't mean it has to happen.' It was a flat, bald statement and she faced him squarely as she said it. 'I can't lease out my body, Conrad. I'm not made like that.'

'If that phone hadn't rung—'

'But it did,' she interrupted with painful determination. Her eyes dropped for a moment, and then as she raised them she went on, 'You are very good at what you do, Conrad—in all aspects of your life. And I can't deny that I…that I am attracted to you physically.'

She wasn't used to speaking about such things and she knew her cheeks were burning.

'But?' he said with lethal control.

'But it isn't enough. Not for me,' she stumbled on. He was going to think she was callow and unsophisticated and pathetic; he'd probably have a good laugh at her expense in a moment and put the final nail in her coffin.

'You want the till-death-us-do-part bit?' he asked incredulously. But he didn't laugh; for that she was eternally grateful. The way she was feeling it would have finished her.

'I don't know what I want,' she answered with a frankness that was disarming, 'but I do know it's not what you are offering. I... Something happened when I was younger and it made me...go into myself, shut down on emotions and men and the whole love thing. Meeting you has made me realise I can't go on like that any more, so that's something.'

'I am so glad.' It was deeply sarcastic and carried a strong note of smarting male ego.

'I want the sort of relationship my mother had with my father,' she said suddenly, his mordant cynicism loosening her tongue. 'They were ecstatically happy together and when he died...well, she didn't want anyone else. She has always said she was lucky enough to have more happiness in a few short years than most people experience in a lifetime, and their relationship made her strong enough to face the years alone rather than take second-best. I want that sort of love or nothing at all.'

'You call that love?' he asked shortly. 'I call it distinctly unhealthy.'

'Exactly.' She passed a tired hand across her face. 'That's what I mean; you see things so differently from me there's no meeting point. You must be able to see that.'

'You call what we just shared no meeting point?'

She had seen this side of him so often over the last months—the razor-sharp mind taking advantage of every unguarded word, every tiny weakness of his opponent—so it shouldn't have surprised her. She drew in a long silent breath before she said, her voice very calm now, 'You could get that and a darn sight more from any one of your women, Conrad. You don't really need me at all. All cats are grey in the dark, isn't that what they say?'

She saw his eyes narrow and sharpen on her face, his hard countenance darkening, but she still found the courage to say everything that needed to be said. 'You imagine you want me because I'm different to your usual diet of beautiful society women who are happy to play musical beds

For once you feel you have had to play the hunter and it's amused the ''primeval—''' here she couldn't stop a note of bitterness colouring her voice for a second before she took another deep steadying breath and went on—'part of you. That's all. You don't care about me as a person, not really.'

'Cut the amateur psychoanalysis,' he grated coldly.

'I bet you even had the restaurant booked tonight, didn't you?' she went on, as though he hadn't spoken. 'First the gift, then the wining and dining, followed by— Well, we both know what you intended it be followed by, don't we, Conrad?'

She was right. She had known it even before she saw her words confirmed in the furious blue eyes. And the pity of it was *he* was right in one respect—she did want him as much as he wanted her, more in fact, because he had lots of women and she only wanted him.

Everything in her had been fighting against his magnetic attraction from day one, but when he had held her, touched her, she had known that she didn't want him to stop, not ever. He could have had her today, right here on the office carpet, where anyone could have walked in and found them. She had been his for the taking. And they said history didn't repeat itself!

A muscle was working in his jaw and she felt pinned to the spot by the brilliant sapphire gaze as she waited for him to respond to the accusation. But when his voice came the content of the words was more shocking than anything she had expected, even from someone as well versed in the cut and thrust of human warfare as Conrad. 'So, I take it I cancel the restaurant?' he drawled with cruel indifference, and then he turned, walking into his office like he had done so many times in the last months and shutting the door on her.

CHAPTER SIX

IF ANYONE had ever told Sephy that Madge Watkins was an angel in disguise she would have laughed in their face.

However, from the moment Sephy walked into Madge's squeaky clean house the next morning that was exactly what Madge became. The elderly spinster took one look at Sephy's wan, bleached face and pink-rimmed eyes—the results of a sleepless night and many tears—and metamorphosed into a maternal cherub.

Whilst her tiny hands busied themselves in making a pot of tea and several rounds of toast—Sephy having admitted she'd had no breakfast before she left—Madge skilfully drew out the full story of what had transpired, and when Sephy broke down in the telling she offered a lavender-scented shoulder for the younger woman to cry on.

Once ensconced in Madge's neat and cosy sitting room in front of a blazing coal fire—Angus on her lap and a cup of tea and a plateful of toast on a little table at the side of her comfy armchair—Sephy felt a little better. Harsh, icy rain was lashing against the windowpanes and the morning was as dark as if dusk was falling, but here inside Madge's home there was a semblance of peace. And she desperately needed that.

Angus had been delighted to see her, and kept up a low, steady rumbling of pleasure once he had established himself on her lap. The warmth of the big cat's furry body and the way he snuggled into her brought a measure of comfort to Sephy's bruised heart. There was something very therapeutic about Angus.

Madge talked of inconsequentialities until the teapot had

been drained and the toast reduced to a few crumbs, and then she came straight to the point. 'You did absolutely right to refuse him, Sephy,' she said firmly, as though the conversation in the kitchen had happened the moment before instead of fifteen minutes ago. 'And I don't say that because I'm an old-fashioned, fuddy-duddy killjoy either,' she added briskly. 'I know what people think of me; old, dried-up spinster who doesn't know what it's all about. But I've had my moments, m'dear, I can tell you.'

Sephy became aware she was sitting with her mouth agape and shut it quickly, but she couldn't have been more surprised if Angus had suddenly woken up and started talking.

'No, the reason I say you are right is because you think too much of him to enter into what must be—because of Conrad's nature—an essentially disastrous affair.'

'What?' Sephy's senses suddenly became heightened to breaking point. Madge's snug little room—with the small, black-leaded grate and red, glowing fire; the mantelshelf with its wooden candle-holders and stout ticking clock; the well-stuffed three-piece suite and elaborately patterned rug in front of the fire—took on a clarity that made the moment timeless.

'You think too much of him, dear.' Madge's voice was very gentle now as she stared into the shocked golden-brown eyes in front of her. 'I've seen it every time you've visited me.'

'No, no...it's...it's not like that,' Sephy stammered before she came to an abrupt halt. It *was* like that. Some time in the last months she had fallen for Conrad Quentin big time. Oh, admit it, a voice in her head challenged scornfully. Say the word! You love him. In spite of all you know about him, you *love* him. Perhaps it had been inevitable from the start, working with him all the hours under the sun and virtually living in his pocket. He was too mesmerising a man, too fascinating and charismatic, for it to have been any different.

Madge sighed, her shrewd but not unkind button eyes tight on Sephy's face as she watched the realisation dawn. 'It's better to face up to it now,' she said quietly. 'He's broken a good few hearts in his time, believe me. Oh, not that he intended to,' she added quickly, as though Sephy had suggested that very thing. 'No, he's always careful to be scrupulously honest about what he can and can't give, but some of the women—especially the more beautiful ones—have thought they could change him, you see. But it just didn't happen.'

A tide of hot colour washed over Sephy's strained face. 'I've never thought that, Madge,' she said through the tightness in her throat. 'I didn't even know he was thinking like he was until last night. I mean, me…' Her voice trailed away.

Madge gave a sudden snort that caused Angus to raise a startled head from Sephy's lap. 'Why not you?' she asked briskly. 'Don't undervalue yourself, Sephy. You've got more of what makes a real woman in your little finger than women like Caroline de Menthe have got in the whole of their bodies.' Madge stopped abruptly, a strange look passing over her face as she stared into Sephy's huge liquid eyes, their thick lashes accentuating the amber tint. 'Who knows?' she said very softly, as if to herself. 'Stranger things have happened. Every man has his own Waterloo.'

'What?' Sephy hadn't been able to catch what Madge had said.

'Nothing.' Madge shook herself, planting her feet firmly on the floor as she raised herself from the chair. 'Right, I'm going to put two baked potatoes and some pork chops in the oven to cook for our lunch, and then we'll get down to those.' She indicated the pile of files Sephy had brought with her. 'And don't worry, m'dear,' she added softly, stopping by Sephy's chair and stroking one smooth cheek for a second. 'You carry on being yourself.'

'Yes, I will.' Sephy stared at her, somewhat bewildered but feeling comforted. There was much more to this little woman than met the eye!

It was gone half past eight before Sephy stood up to leave the benign confines of Madge's small home, and then only after a delicious tea of hot toasted muffins and homemade strawberry jam.

For most of the long winter afternoon the two women had just sat in front of the fire and chatted about all sorts of things, and it wasn't until Sephy was driving home in the taxi—which Conrad had previously insisted she take both ways and charge to the company—that she realised Madge had confided far more about Conrad than she'd appreciated at the time.

The stark, utilitarian existence he had been forced to endure at boarding school from the age of seven, which had aimed at a rigid, army-like discipline; his difficult teenage years when he had fought against authority at school and rebelled at being shipped from pillar to post among his relatives in the holidays; the pain he still felt about his sister's untimely death, and much more besides.

'He's carved a name for himself. Quite literally carved it, with his blood, sweat and tears,' Madge had said pensively, adding with a wry smile, 'No, forget the tears. He told me once, oh, years ago now, that he can't remember the last time he cried—it wasn't encouraged, either at home or at the school, to show emotion, you see. If he'd been mine it would have been different.'

'You look on him as a son, don't you?' Sephy had said gently, and the elderly woman had nodded slowly.

'I was fifty years old when Conrad engaged me as his secretary over a host of young things with degrees and what have you,' Madge had said softly. 'I'd been made redundant, and it seemed like everyone had written me off because of my age, and then Conrad gave me a chance. He said he believed in me, in my experience and wisdom over material qualifications. One minute I was an old has-been everyone was treating with contempt, the next... Yes, I look upon him as my lad. I can't help it.'

He had been wonderful to Madge, the little woman had related incident after incident to prove it, so why couldn't he extend the milk of human kindness to the rest of the human race? Sephy asked herself as she looked out of the taxi's steaming window into the gray sleety rain outside. There had been times this afternoon when she had found herself envying the lonely, solitary little old woman, and if that didn't make her the saddest person in London she didn't know what did! A self-mocking, mordacious smile brushed her soft lips.

Anyway, the most unlikely affair in the whole of history was over before it had even begun! She had to put this behind her, concentrate on her job and perhaps even consider moving companies to further her career. The boost the last few months had made to her CV wasn't to be sneezed at, and besides—her mouth drooped unknowingly as street after sleet-drenched street flashed by outside—she couldn't continue working at Quentin Dynamics now.

Conrad had talked about her getting under his skin, but he had done something much more ruthless. He had taken her heart, stolen it under the guise of familiarity and comradeship and everything else working together so closely had embodied. She hadn't *wanted* to fall in love with him but it had happened nevertheless. And now she could understand what had made him the way he was, could feel compassion and tenderness and a thousand other emotions besides, it made him much more dangerous if he did but know it. She couldn't risk any contact with him. That was it in a nutshell.

By the time the taxi drew up outside Jerry's menswear shop the situation had clarified as coldly as the icy weather outside. Which made it all the more devastating when—the second the taxi drew away and she hurried towards the flat entrance, her head down against the stinging torrent—a deep, dark, husky voice spoke her name.

She swung round just in time to see Conrad's big, lean body moving towards her, the Mercedes parked on the opposite side of the road, and she froze. She just froze.

'Hello, Sephy.' It was cool, cold even, but the sensual impact of those stunning blue eyes was undiminished. 'I expected you home long before this,' he said as he reached her side.

She could have said any one of a number of things to defuse—or at least steer—the conversation, all of which came to her with hindsight, but instead she found herself staring at him with huge shocked eyes as the driving sleet enveloped them in an icy blanket. And still she couldn't speak.

'Where have you been?' His voice was impassive but his gaze was intent on her reaction. 'It's late.'

'You know.' And then, as his face didn't change, 'I've been to Madge's, of course. That's what you ordered, isn't it?' she said with a sudden burst of anger.

'Right.' He looked at her for a long moment which seemed endless and then he moved closer, to tower over her. 'You've been there all day?' he said calmly. 'Until now?'

'We had lunch.' She was trying to pull herself together and sound matter-of-fact but he just looked so *gorgeous*. 'And then tea. And we talked some.'

'Lunch and tea.' He was surprised, she knew it, and, knowing Madge's reputation for keeping all her subordinates ruthlessly in their place, it perhaps wasn't surprising.

'And she's invited me for Sunday lunch,' Sephy couldn't

resist adding, as a little demon of pride urged, Show him, show him you aren't like all the rest as far as his esteemed Madge is concerned at least!

'Has she?' He nodded slowly. 'Well, well, well. That's quite an honour if you did but know it. Madge is a tough old bird; she's had to be with the sort of knocks life's dished out in her direction.'

Sephy gazed at him uncertainly. She had to guard herself against him; she *had* to. If he sensed any weakness in her, any irresolution, he would pounce. The more she got to know about this man the more she realised the very words he had just said about Madge applied to him. Deep inside somewhere, hidden under layers and layers of steel cladding, was an emotionally scarred individual who was as vulnerable and scared of being rejected as the next person. But if she allowed her love to override her common sense it would be nothing short of emotional suicide.

She didn't know what it would take for someone to break through the hurt of thirty-eight years—some sort of a miracle, probably—or even if anyone *could*, but she would have to be a pretty special woman, that was for sure. Caroline de Menthe and all his other beauties rolled into one and then some.

She, herself, didn't have a clue how to reach him and wouldn't stand a chance of surviving a relationship with him. David Bainbridge had been a spoilt, selfish brat of a boy. The person she had thought she loved had never existed except in her girlish imagination. Conrad Quentin was a man, an emotionally damaged, hard, ruthless man, and even knowing all that she loved him.

He was momentarily attracted to her because he found her different. She had stood up to him to start with, and then refused to jump into bed with him when he had expected it. She was a novelty, a curiosity; her self-confessed lack of interest in the male species had probably been something of a challenge to him to begin with. Men were like that. But he would tire of her immediately she became his.

Sephy took a deep breath and said quietly, 'Why are you here, Conrad? I thought we had said all there was to say yesterday at the office. I don't want to argue with you again.'

'Can we talk inside?' He raised his hand to her hair, which was now wringing wet. 'We're both getting soaked out here.'

She felt her stomach turn over but managed to say, fairly steadily, 'I don't think that's a good idea,' as she jerked away from his touch. 'I think it's better if you go, don't you?'

Now his strong hands cupped her damp face and the blue eyes were relentless. 'I want to talk to you, Sephy, and you know me well enough by now to know that I don't take no for an answer. We can have this conversation in my car, at my house, in your flat, a pub, wherever. But have it we will, and I refuse to let you get pneumonia because of a childish determination to prove a point.'

His arrogance provided a welcome shot of adrenalin that put some force in her hands as she pushed him away, and fire in her eyes. 'You think you've always got to win, don't you? Always get your own way?' she hissed furiously.

'Exactly.' And he had the nerve to smile mockingly. 'So, that accepted, defiance is useless. Now, where is it to be?'

'It is to be nowhere,' she spat, with a disregard for grammar and lucidity. 'Just leave me alone, will you?'

And it might have been all right, he might have gone, if Jerry hadn't chosen that precise moment to call to her from the doorway of his shop. 'Sephy? Everything all right?'

Sephy groaned inwardly even before she saw Conrad's face stiffen and his eyes become pinpoints of blue ice as he turned slightly to face the shop. 'What the hell is it to do with you?' he asked with lethal control.

Considering that Conrad was considerably broader and a few inches taller than the other man, and right at this moment seemed even more so with the rage that had tightened his powerful body and darkened his features, Sephy thought Jerry was incredibly brave when he said, without a quiver, 'I'm Sephy's friend, so it's everything to do with me if she's being hassled.'

'*Hassled?*'

Conrad had actually taken a step towards the figure in the doorway when Sephy grabbed his arm, her voice urgent as she looked across at Jerry and said, 'It's fine, really. Conrad's come to discuss a problem at work.' *Why had Jerry had to work late tonight?*

'The hell Conrad has!' Conrad said grimly. 'I've come here to see Sephy, and the whys and wherefores are between the two of us, okay? Clear enough for you?'

'Sephy?'

Jerry's nice brown eyes focused on her face, and she found herself nodding somewhat frantically, like one of those toy dogs with bobbing heads in the backs of cars. 'It's all right, Jerry. It really is all right. Please, you go in. I mean it.'

She could feel the bunched muscles under her hand as she hung on to Conrad's arm and she knew it wouldn't take much for the situation to spiral way out of control.

'We're…we're just going to go for a drive,' she improvised rapidly. 'Conrad has come to pick me up.'

'Followed by dinner,' Conrad added silkily. 'Right, Sephy?'

He didn't miss a trick! Sephy forced a smile as she kept her gaze on Jerry, sensing the younger man was still concerned. 'And to get something to eat,' she agreed as steadily as she could. 'Please, you go in. You'll get frozen out here.'

'Well, if you're sure...' Jerry muttered unhappily.

'She's sure.' It was icy-cold and dismissive, and in the next instant Sephy found herself being steered towards the waiting Mercedes.

She had assumed Conrad was driving himself, as he did when the mood took him, so it was something of a shock as she neared the car to see the impassive figure of James in the driving seat. Oh, great! Just great! He probably hadn't heard anything but he must have gathered plenty from the little scene outside the window, Sephy thought tightly. It didn't take much for rumours to start at work and she'd lay good money on what the next one would be!

Conrad opened the door for her and she slid into the rear of the car with as much dignity as her dripping state would allow. He followed a second later, and she forced herself not to stiffen or react in any way as his dark bulk seemed to fill the Mercedes.

'Back to the office, James.' His voice was expressionless, uninterested even. 'And then you can go; I'll get a taxi home. Pick me up in the morning at...' He considered for a second. 'Nine. Okay?'

'Yes, Mr Quentin.'

Very nicely done. Sephy kept her eyes on the back of James's immaculate neck as she sat stiffly at Conrad's side. To all intents and purposes he had picked her up to go back to the office to work; his consideration of her reputation was priceless in the circumstances!

She didn't know whether to feel angry or touched that Conrad had bothered to try and protect her good name, but in view of all he had said regarding his openly predatory designs she decided on the former. Hypocrite! She repeated the word a few times for good measure, feeding her outrage.

He thought he had manoeuvred things all his own way, as usual, but she was blowed if she was going to be relegated to that section of his mind labelled 'crumpet', along with all the others. If nothing else he would remember Sephy Vincent as the one who wouldn't play ball when he snapped those impossibly arrogant fingers.

She sat quietly at his side as the powerful car cut its way through the late-evening traffic, and Conrad made no effort to break the silence. She was hotly aware of him; the big black overcoat on the perimeter of her vision, the intoxicating sensual smell of his aftershave, the animal warmth of his big body in the limited confines of the car. But she forced herself to stare out of the side window as though his presence didn't disturb her at all. He didn't have the monopoly on cool remoteness!

James stopped outside the main entrance of Quentin Dynamics, and after Conrad had thanked the chauffeur and told him to stay in the car he walked round himself to open her door.

'Thank you.' She exited with her head held high and her eyes straight ahead, although the rat's tails hanging round her face spoilt the effect somewhat.

The building was all but deserted when they entered it, just a few cleaners going about their business in the empty offices, and as Conrad began to walk towards the lift Sephy stopped him in his tracks as she said, 'You don't need to call a taxi for where we're going to eat; it's only a few minutes' walk away.'

He stopped, turning very slowly to face her, and piercing blue eyes narrowed. 'Meaning?'

'Meaning this is my treat,' she said brightly, wondering if he knew how devastating he looked when he adopted that forbidding, sexy, masculine expression.

'Your...?' He stared at her as though she'd spoken in Chinese.

'Treat, yes.' And put that in your pipe and smoke it. 'If I remember rightly you gave me dinner at your home the last time, so it's only right I treat you now. There's a great little Italian place that Jerry found—' She stopped abruptly as the blue gaze became laser-bright. 'Where a bunch of us go to eat quite regularly. It's clean, the prices are reasonable and the cannelloni *ripieni* is out of this world.' It was also extremely basic, and not at all the place a multimillionaire would ever be found dead in.

'And it's your treat,' he said very flatly.

It was sticking in his craw, and much as she loved him Sephy relished the fact. She nodded briskly as she said, 'Take it or leave it.'

'Oh, I take it. I most certainly take it,' he drawled lazily, something in his eyes making a tiny shudder of sensation curl through every vein and sinew and remind her that she was playing with fire. And fire had a way of getting out of control too fast.

'Good.' She gulped silently. 'It's halfway between here and the flat, so it's only a five-minute walk.'

He glanced over her shoulder, surveying the weather, which had worsened—if that was possible—in the last few minutes, and then let his eyes run over her wet hair, which was drying in tiny curls around her face where it had become loosened from the knot at the back of her head. She didn't flinch at his mocking perusal.

'I'm sure Reception won't miss this.' He bent over the beautifully stained wood desk that ran in a large semicircle at one side of the lobby and extracted a huge courtesy umbrella from its hiding place. 'There's room enough for two under here.'

The words were innocuous enough; it was the tone of his husky voice that made her shiver.

She was ashamed of the weakness, she really was, but Sephy found herself wishing the walk to the restaurant could have lasted for ever. It was the sort of stuff dreams were made of.

As they stepped out of the centrally heated warmth of the foyer into the harsh, driving sleet Conrad folded her securely into his side, one arm round her shoulders and the other holding the massive umbrella protectively over her so that they were enclosed in their own intimate world.

Her head slid just under his square chin, as though it had been made to fit there, and the angle at which he was holding her forced her arm round his waist so that her stomach was pressed against his hard thigh and the smell and feel of him was all around her.

'Mmm, this was a good idea of yours after all.' His voice was deep and husky as they stood just outside the building, careless of the harassed commuters hurrying past them, anxious to catch buses and trains. 'I never realised what I was missing using the car all these years.'

One of his other women would have made some light, teasing, amusing reply, no doubt, but held against his powerful male body as she was, with trickles of heat making her limbs fluid, Sephy thought she was doing pretty well just to remain upright.

He didn't love her, and his interest was predacious to say the least, but her body seemed determined to ignore all the frantic warnings her brain was giving it and thrill to his closeness. Her breasts were heavy and full, there was a warm throbbing ache deep inside her and her blood was singing through her veins in a way that made her feel more gloriously alive than she had in years.

'Five minutes, did you say?' He whispered the words into her hair, lowering his head slightly, and she felt herself go weak at the knees. 'How about we go the long way?'

'I...I don't know a long way,' she said feebly.

'Pity.'

He lowered his head further, his eyes moving over her

flushed cheeks and bright eyes, and then he smiled, very slowly, his gaze warm on her face. 'Eyes like warm honey. Eyes a man could lose himself in,' he murmured softly. 'I've never seen such eyes before. And your skin is real peaches and cream.'

'We…we ought to start walking.' If they didn't she would melt into a little pool at his feet and he would have to scoop her up off the pavement.

'You're beautiful, Sephy, and you really don't know it, do you?' he continued in a low voice. 'I've watched you over the last months—hell, I've done nothing else but watch you all day and take umpteen cold showers all night—and you're genuinely oblivious to how you effect the male sex.'

She stared at him in utter surprise, the eyes of which he had spoken open wide and her mouth slightly agape. He couldn't seriously be talking about her, could he? Was he mad?

She couldn't let him guess what this was doing to her. She drew on all her reserves and managed to say, her voice faintly teasing, 'Cold showers? With Caroline and all those other gorgeous women available? I think not.'

The stunning blue eyes were very steady as he said, 'My position makes it necessary to have companions at various functions and whatever, but since the first day you have worked for me that's all they have been. I have never yet taken one woman to bed for mere sexual release when my mind and my body has been occupied with someone else. Even I have certain principles.'

'You weren't occupied with me,' she protested shakily.

'Oh, yes, I was, Sephy,' he said softly, a strange half-smile on his lips. 'More than you'll ever know.'

This powerful, magnetic, ruthless tycoon, who could inspire fear and trembling in the most hard-boiled business associates and have women falling at his feet in seconds, had been waiting for her? It was unbelievable, and yet in all the months she had known him she had never heard him lie.

'You accused me of playing musical beds and that assumption is based on gossip and hearsay,' he continued quietly. 'Whilst it wasn't particularly flattering to think you considered me that crass, I could understand where it had come from. I've had women, Sephy, lots of women, from the time I ventured out into the big bad world, but if I'd slept with all the females accredited to me I'd deserve a medal for sheer endurance. I can actually take a woman out for the pleasure of her company and nothing else.'

She stared up into the dark lean face, totally unaware of anything but him.

'I'm rich and I'm powerful and those attributes carry their own penalties,' Conrad said evenly. 'There's always some reporter somewhere who's anxious to fill a column, and if they can get under your skin a bit, rile you, then all the better. Human nature is the same the whole world over, and the have-nots will always take a hit at the ones who have made it, even if they've sweated blood to get there.'

'And have you sweated blood?' she asked softly.

They looked at each other for a second and then he shrugged dismissively. 'There were a few rough times in the beginning, but I can't complain,' he said, in such a way she knew the brief glimpse into the psyche of this complicated and disturbing man was over. He allowed her so far and then no more, and it was tantalising.

'So…' He pulled her closer in to him as he lowered the massive umbrella a fraction and kissed her swiftly before straightening again. 'I'm in your hands,' he said silkily, his eyes lazy.

'My hands?' Brief as the kiss had been, it had caused feelings akin to little flames flickering through her.

'The way to the restaurant?' he mocked softly. 'Remember?'

'Oh, yes, of course.' She tried to pull herself together but it wasn't easy, locked against him as she was. And he knew, he *knew* how he was affecting her, she told herself silently, but just at the moment she couldn't work up the annoyance his arrogance should have demanded. Not with him holding her like this.

Time lost all meaning on the short walk to Giorgio's. She had never felt so cherished, so protected, so deliciously feminine in her life before, and even though she knew it was an illusion—at least the cherishing part—it didn't stop her from feeling as though she'd entered heaven on earth.

The little restaurant was almost full when Conrad opened the door and she stepped into the warm, aromatic interior— Giorgio was beginning to benefit from a well-deserved reputation and inevitably Friday nights were always popular— but when Giorgio saw her he at once came bustling to their side, his round face beaming.

'We haven't booked,' Sephy said quickly, before he asked, 'but I wondered if you'd got a table for two, Giorgio?'

'For you, my beautiful lady, anything,' Giorgio enthused in his heavy accent, before turning to Conrad and saying, 'This lovely lady, she is beautiful, *si*? I tell her all the time.'

'Very beautiful,' Conrad agreed, 'and I tell her too.'

'This is good, verrry good.' The smile became beatific. 'You give me your coats and I take you to my verrry best table, *si*?'

Once they were seated in the far corner of the restaurant, and Giorgio had given them a somewhat dog-eared menu along with further effusive compliments for Sephy, she leant forward and said very quietly, 'He calls all the women beautiful; he's Italian.'

'I'm English, and I agree with him in this instance.'

She stared at him, wondering if he knew how incongruous his designer suit and handmade shoes looked in the spartan confines of Giorgio's scruffy little restaurant. He didn't appear to, in fact he seemed perfectly relaxed and at home, but then Conrad never gave anything away. An enigma, that was what he was. A unique, twenty-four-carat enigma, with blue eyes and a smile to die for.

When the food came it was as good as Sephy had promised, and the raspberry-flavoured dry red wine Conrad had insisted on ordering and paying for was excellent, although wildly expensive.

'I didn't know he had wines like this,' Sephy gulped in surprise after her first taste. 'But then we always go for the cheap plonk, I'm afraid. Giorgio must despair at times.'

'We?' Conrad queried smoothly.

'There's a gang of us who normally come once or twice a week.'

'Right.' Narrowed blue eyes surveyed her thoughtfully for a moment. 'Well, let me tell you your Giorgio knows his wines,' Conrad said pleasantly. 'This place is quite a little find.'

Was he being patronising? Sephy asked herself silently, before she admitted she was being unfair. He was enjoying himself, it was patently obvious, and it wasn't exactly what she had expected. It wasn't very uplifting to admit she was capable of such mean-mindedness but she had to acknowledge she had hoped, deep inside, that he would display some disdain or superciliousness—anything—to bring to light a deficit in his character. She needed something to dislike him for, and snobbishness was as good as anything else.

She looked at him as he sat back in his chair, sipping his wine and gazing around the small restaurant, and her heart lurched and then raced on like an express train. She could still hardly believe she was here with him like this, or that yesterday evening had happened. Her and Conrad? It was surreal, impossible.

'What's the matter?' As the piercing eyes fastened on her face she realised, too late, that he had been aware of her scrutiny.

'The matter? Why does anything have to be the matter?' she parried quickly, knowing she was blushing a bright red.

There was a significant little silence as he gave her a long, meaningful look. 'Because you are you,' he said drily, 'and I'm learning fast. What have I done wrong this time?'

'Don't be silly. You haven't done anything wrong.'

She was immensely glad that Giorgio chose that particular moment to come bustling up to remove their empty plates and give them the dessert menu. He didn't often wait on customers, his two daughters were employed in that role, but he seemed to have taken a liking to Conrad—or more probably a liking to his obvious wealth, Sephy thought a trifle cynically. Giorgio was a businessman first and foremost.

'Wow.' Conrad glanced at the handwritten menu before looking at Sephy, his eyes smiling. 'Can I choose anything I like?' he asked humbly, his eyes gently mocking her.

'Of course.' Her voice was stiff; she couldn't help it.

'Then I'll have a double portion of the tiramisu,' Conrad said with open unrepentant greed, 'and, as I'm not driving, a liqueur coffee to follow. French, I think.'

'Ah, this is good. A man who knows what he likes,' Giorgio gushed at their side.

And then Sephy went a brilliant pink as Conrad said softly, his eyes fixed on her flushed face, 'Oh, I know what I like, but not everything is as easy to get as the tiramisu.'

'Yes, well, I'll have the caramel orange, please,' Sephy cut in quickly, her voice something of a snap as she lowered her eyes to the menu in her hands. 'And just coffee with cream, Giorgio.'

For the rest of the meal Conrad put himself out to be amusing and charming, and Sephy thought he had forgotten their previous conversation, but then, having paid the bill among more ebullient profusion from Giorgio, they stepped into the dark, cold world beyond the restaurant doors. It had stopped sleeting but the winter night was freezing, the sky covered by dense cloud, and they had only gone a few steps towards the flat when Conrad turned her to face him. He looked down at her, his blue eyes narrowed and thoughtful.

'I want to know,' he said softly.

'Know?' She stared up at him, genuinely at a loss.

'What you were thinking of in there before Giorgio came up with the dessert menu,' he said evenly. 'Were you comparing me with him? With this guy who broke your heart?'

'I've never said anyone broke my heart,' Sephy protested hotly. She didn't want to do this, and especially not right now.

'Who was he, Sephy?' His voice was harsher now, tight even. 'This ''something'' that happened to you when you were younger that you spoke of? Did he abuse you, was that it? Or was it a love affair that ended badly? Did you live with him?' he pressed further.

Sephy was stunned. 'What? No, of course I didn't live with him,' she said unthinkingly, before coming to an abrupt halt.

'In this day and age there is no ''of course'' about it,' he said tersely.

'There is for me.' She tried to remove herself from his grasp but his grip on her forearms tightened. 'It was nothing like that.'

'So, tell me.' His eyes were holding hers, their blue blinding.

'There's nothing to tell,' she said defensively. And there wasn't, not really. 'He, David, was just a boy I knew in the place where I grew up. I thought he liked me, he didn't, so that was that. It happens all the time in one way or another. End of story.'

He let go of one of her arms, but only so he could cup her small jaw. 'The hell it is,' he said softly. 'He hurt you badly, didn't he, this David. Put you off the male sex for a long time?'

She shrugged, showing him her pure sweet profile as she looked away. 'It happens,' she said stiffly. 'It's history now anyway.'

'How old were you?'

'Eighteen.' Oh, God, please make him stop asking these probing questions, she prayed silently. She couldn't tell him all of it; she would rather die. A broken love affair was one thing; there was at least some street cred in that. But what had happened to her was just debasing and humiliating and horrible. And he was a man who had had hundreds of women; his experience was vast and his mind was blasé and sophisticated. He would find it laughable that she had allowed it to happen in the first place, and be incredulous that it had continued to affect her up to this present time. What would he say if he knew she had *never* had a steady boyfriend, just the odd date now and again?

'Eighteen.' Anger thickened his voice and he swore, a raw profanity that shocked Sephy into lowering her thick lashes and jerking away. She couldn't talk about this any more.

'Please, Conrad...' She took a silent pull of the icy air and forced her voice to be steady. 'I don't want to talk about this, okay?'

'Okay.' He reached out and pulled her roughly into his arms, his voice controlled again. 'I'm sorry he hurt the young eighteen-year-old Sephy,' he said quietly, his voice deep and sincere, and with a note in it that brought her head up to meet his eyes. He touched her mouth tenderly with one finger as he added, 'But if he hadn't, you might have settled for boring domesticity instead of turning into the career woman you are now, and then we wouldn't have met.'

Career woman. She felt a sharp stab as guilt pierced her conscience. All this, to him chasing her and everything that had happened, was because she had misled him from the start. She wasn't a career woman. Not in the way he assumed anyway—the way all his other women were. Boring domesticity—she would give the rest of her life for a day of boring domesticity with him. And he would run a mile if he knew that! This was all suddenly very muddled.

She knew he was going to kiss her and she had never wanted anything so much in her life. Nevertheless she stiffened, attempting to pull away, but then she was crushed against him in the dark shadows of the badly lit street and his lips moved against hers, dominating and hungry.

And immediately, without any warning, she felt the desire rise up in her with such desperate need that she sagged against him slightly as his whole body seemed to enclose her.

He was too good at this; that was the trouble. The warning thought was there, but it did nothing to help. He was too tender, too sensual, too strong, too powerful to resist, and dangerous. Frighteningly dangerous. Excitingly and thrillingly dangerous.

Her head had fallen back as she'd instinctively allowed him even greater access to the sweet confines of her mouth, and he swiftly drained her response, taking everything, until she was limp and trembling against him.

'Come on.' His breathing was ragged and not quite steady when he at last lifted his head and released her. 'Let's get you home.'

Home? She stared at him for a second, utterly unable to pull herself together, and then he tucked her arm in his and forced her to begin walking along the wet, shiny pavement, the dull, opaque glow from the street lamp at the corner of the road making a soft circle of gold on the ground.

What would it be like if he *really* began to make love to her? She almost missed her footing, and his arm tightened as he drew her more securely against his protective bulk. If his kisses could reduce her to this, what would she feel then? Heaven. Heaven on earth—devastating, shattering, fantastic.

And when he left? a separate part of her brain asked coldly. Because he *would* leave; he had already told her so. An affair with Conrad would be a finite thing, subject to tight limitations even as it happened. He would terminate their liaison as he terminated certain business deals; swiftly and without regret.

She shivered, but it was nothing to do with the bitterly cold night air and all to do with the brief glimpse her heart had revealed of a bleak, hopeless, unthinkable future. He would eat her up and spit her out and she wouldn't even leave a taste in his mouth. He wouldn't set out to hurt her, she believed that, but the end result would be the same.

And it was that vision that enabled her to say, once they reached the door leading up to her flat, 'Thanks for tonight, Conrad,' in a tone that was intentionally dismissive as she extracted her arm from his. 'I've enjoyed it.'

'It should be me thanking you,' he said quietly, his eyes glinting down at her. 'You paid for the meal.'

'But you paid for the wine and it was as much as the food,' she returned smilingly, determined to keep it light and easy.

'I gather I'm not being asked up for coffee?' He didn't sound particularly concerned about it, and perversely it caught her on the raw. It was no trouble for him to take her or leave her.

She didn't trust her voice not to betray what she was feeling so she merely shook her head coolly.

And to her surprise he didn't try to persuade her. He didn't even attempt to kiss her goodnight, he merely nodded, his voice pleasant but somewhat remote as he said, 'Goodnight, Sephy.'

That was it? She stared at him as he turned away with an easy smile and began walking down the street. After all he'd said and that kiss outside Giorgio's that was it? He was leaving?

Too late she remembered he had said to James he would call a taxi to take him home; she should have offered the use of her phone at least. He would think her so boorish.

Without even thinking about it she called after him, 'The taxi! Do you want to come up for a minute and call a taxi?'

'Don't worry, I've got my mobile with me.' He patted the big pocket of his overcoat as he spoke, but his stride didn't falter or check in any way and neither did he turn round.

And then he had reached the corner of the road and disappeared from view, still without looking back, and she was suddenly alone. And she felt alone, desperately alone.

She stood in the shadow of Jerry's shop doorway for a full minute without moving as a dark, consuming heaviness fell over her like a blanket. She felt bitterly disappointed and tired and drained—exhausted with too many emotions she couldn't handle or even define. But all connected with Conrad Quentin.

She had fought her own battles and overcome her own problems for years, and she knew that was what she had to keep on doing, that her stand against Conrad was right, but just at this precise moment she would have given the world for it all to be different. For *him* to be different.

But he wasn't. She raised her head and stared up into

the sky just as a scudding cloud revealed a brief glimpse of the white ethereal beauty of the crescent moon.

And tonight had told her one thing. She had to leave Quentin Dynamics, and soon, because if she didn't, if she allowed him into her life and ultimately her body, he would destroy her.

CHAPTER SEVEN

SEPHY was awoken early the next morning—after a night of continuous tossing and turning and weird, disturbing dreams—by the sound of the buzzer to her flat being pressed repeatedly.

She stumbled into the little hall, fastening the belt of her robe as she went, and spoke into the intercom in a voice still thick with sleep. 'Yes, who is it?'

'Delivery for Miss Vincent.' The female voice was young and bright and impossibly cheery for this early on a Saturday morning.

She was too dazed and drowsy to wonder what the delivery could be as she opened the flat door and stumbled down the stairs to the outer door into the street, but when she opened it and the most enormous bouquet was placed in her hands by a smiling, chirpy delivery girl it acted in the same way as a bucket of cold water straight in her sleepy face and suddenly she was wide awake.

'Have a nice day.' The pretty young face was openly envious as the girl glanced once more at the dozens of red roses and fragile baby's breath the Cellophane held. 'And, whoever he is, he's sure no cheapskate,' she added perkily over her shoulder as she turned towards the florist's van parked at the edge of the kerb.

'It's serious, then?'

Sephy came out of her mesmerised state to find Jerry peering at her as the van drove off into the mounting morning traffic, and when he indicated the flowers she felt her face turn as red as the roses. Jerry had a way of always being around at the wrong time.

'It's not like that, really,' she said quickly.

'Oh, Sephy.' He shook his head at her, his nice face deeply troubled. 'I saw the way he looked at you.'

After the foul weather of the night before the January morning was crisp and bright but bitterly cold, and as its icy chill quickly penetrated her thick towelling robe she shivered before saying, her voice flat, 'He's the original love 'em and leave 'em type, Jerry, and I don't go in for emotional suicide, besides which I don't work for him any more—his old secretary's back, and I'm thinking of leaving the firm.'

He nodded slowly. 'Sounds sensible,' he said quietly, 'and Maisie will be glad to hear you might be around a bit more. We've missed you.' He smiled at her, his face open and friendly.

There was an inflexion in the 'we' that made her ask, 'You two are getting on well, then?'

'Very well.' It was warm and said far more than just the mere words indicated. 'We might even make it permanent.'

'I'm glad.' She smiled at him and his smile widened, but as she stepped inside and closed the door she suddenly felt painfully alone in a way she hadn't done for years. Which was stupid—really, *really* stupid, she told herself bracingly as she hurried up the stairs to the snug warmth of the flat, because nothing had changed. And she and Jerry would never have worked in a million years.

She laid the flowers on the breakfast bar and then, as a thought occurred to her, she reached for the little envelope attached to the Cellophane. She, along with Jerry, had assumed the flowers had come from Conrad, but they might not have. Although she couldn't think of another person on the whole earth who would send her flowers—and so extravagantly!

'They are soft and beautiful and sweetly perfumed, just

like you,' he had written. 'But the thorns warn one to handle with respect, just like... C.'

Handle with respect! How could he be so manipulative and machiavellian and...and *hypocritical*? she asked herself furiously, before bursting into tears.

She felt better after a good cry, and once the roses were in water—all five dozen of them—she soaked in a hot bath for over an hour without letting her mind consider the future once.

She had just dried her hair into soft thick waves about her face, and was considering getting dressed, when the buzzer sounded again. It was going to be one of those mornings!

Maisie. It had to be Maisie. No doubt Jerry had related the latest and she had popped round to get the 'i's dotted and the 't's crossed, as was Maisie's wont, Sephy thought patiently. She flicked the switch on the intercom and said flatly, 'Okay, Maisie, a coffee and a croissant, right?' Whenever Maisie did this she always arrived with half a dozen croissants and a sweetly entreating smile and never failed to gain admittance.

'I've never been called Maisie before—' the darkly amused voice was deep and husky and made her heart jump into her mouth '—and I'm right out of croissants.'

'Conrad?' He was here, *now*, and she must look such a *mess*.

'Sorry to disappoint you if you're hungry,' he said drily.

He was here, right now! She glanced in the hall mirror and inwardly groaned. Her face was shiny, her eyes still carried the penalty of the good cry and she was only clothed in her nightie beneath the robe. Don't panic, Sephy, she told herself desperately.

'What...what do you want?' she stammered at last, somewhat ungraciously, before adding, 'Thank you for the flowers.'

'My pleasure.' There was something so sexy about his husky voice it made her toes curl, which, no doubt, was *exactly* what he intended, she told herself caustically. Tried and tested formula.

She took a deep breath but her voice still carried a faint tremor as she repeated, 'What do you want, Conrad?'

'You.'

She swallowed hard. Okay, she should have expected that.

'But then you know that,' he drawled mockingly. 'Don't you?'

'I'm...I'm not dressed yet,' she said, before she considered her words.

'And they say there isn't a Santa Claus.'

'Conrad, *please*.' She glanced again in the mirror and groaned.

'I want to take you out to lunch, Sephy, or is that a terrible crime?' he asked softly, but this time there was a thread of naked steel running through the words that she recognised from her time as his secretary. It told her he wasn't going to take no for an answer.

'I might have other plans,' she managed after a few frantic moments. But she was only prolonging the inevitable.

'Have you?' He clearly wasn't buying that one.

Some deep feminine instinct for self-preservation urged her to say yes, but the thought of a few hours with him was too tempting. Lunch was safe, nothing could happen during lunch, and she had already made the decision to leave Quentin Dynamics at the earliest opportunity. She deserved this day. She did. It was all she was likely to ever have.

She had hesitated too long, and now his voice was very dry when he said, 'Get dressed, Sephy, and be downstairs in ten minutes or I'll upset your friend—Jerry, isn't it?—by breaking this door down.'

'Don't be ridiculous,' she said indignantly. 'You wouldn't dare.'

'I'm never ridiculous, and just try me.'

It was arrogant and cold and so very Conrad that it made her smile in spite of the circumstances, but she managed to keep all trace of amusement out of her voice as she said tersely, 'Fifteen minutes, and don't you dare so much as touch that door.'

She put the phone down on his warm throaty chuckle but the ache of longing it caused was harder to control.

They lunched at a small old-fashioned inn in Stratford-upon-Avon, where the steak pie cooked in Guinness was wonderful and the raspberry pavlova was homemade and melted in the mouth.

The drive out had been leisurely, and Conrad appeared perfectly relaxed, but from the moment she had caught sight of him as she had stepped on to the pavement Sephy had felt her nerves pull as tight as piano wire.

She had never seen him dressed casually before, he had always worn any one of a number of beautifully cut designer suits for the office, but today his black denim jeans and waist-length bulky charcoal-grey leather jacket emphasised his dark, virile masculinity a hundredfold and it made her—quite literally—weak at the knees. He was intimidatingly sexy and flagrantly male from the top of his ebony head to the soles of his shoes, and she felt she had caught a tiger by the tail. Although she hadn't caught him, she reminded herself silently, she hadn't remotely caught him, and therein lay the root of all her problems. He was a law unto himself and answerable to no one.

'What would you like to do for the rest of the day?' he asked lazily as they finished their coffee, his vivid blue eyes moving over her silky dark hair which she had left loose to fall in soft waves about her shoulders. 'We don't need to be back in London until sevenish, but I've booked a table at the Calypso Club for eight-thirty and no doubt you'll want time to put on your glad rags.'

She stared at him uncertainly. Rarely a week or two went by when some glossy magazine or other didn't have pictures of a host of celebrities enjoying themselves at the Calypso. It was the place to be seen, the haunt of the jet-set and the beautiful people, and you had to be worth a mint just to step inside its exclusive doors. This was so far outside her league as to be laughable. She had to make him understand.

'Conrad, this isn't going to work,' she said as firmly as she could. 'You do see that, don't you? All I said...I still mean it.'

'You mean about prostituting yourself or my seeing you just as a challenge?' he queried with shocking impassivity. 'Or perhaps you're referring to your accusation that I don't care about you as a person?' he added, his eyes watching her closely.

Oh, hell! She suddenly realised her words had cut deep. 'I...I shouldn't have said some of that,' she admitted awkwardly.

'No, you're right, you shouldn't,' he said calmly.

'But some of it was true,' she declared tersely. 'Your view on life is so different to mine that we're poles apart—'

'Cut the baloney, Sephy. At least say it as it is.'

Her breath caught painfully in her throat. Beneath the smooth, amusing, controlled exterior this was one angry man.

'You don't trust me; that's it in a nutshell,' he said coolly. 'You've listened to rumour and innuendo.'

'No, that is *not* it,' she shot back quickly, a welcome flood of anger dispelling the momentary guilt and confusion. 'You told me what to expect if I got involved with you and I don't like it, okay? Not every woman wants a wham-bam-thank-you-ma'am kind of love affair, Conrad.'

'A *what*?' Dark colour flared across hard cheekbones and the sparks in his blue eyes warned her it wouldn't take much for the smouldering rage to flare into a blazing fire.

'I'm not capable of going into a relationship knowing it is destined to fail,' Sephy said wretchedly. 'That's what I mean.'

'Who's talking about failure?' he ground out. 'Just because a couple move on to other partners it doesn't mean they have to part acrimoniously or that what they shared is spoilt. My exes have always been quite happy and reasonable when the time has come for us to go our separate ways.'

'How would you know that?' she dared to challenge. 'How would you *know*? You lay down the ground rules; you control the whole thing from beginning to end; you never let anyone get close to you! How would you really *know* what the other person is feeling? You fool yourself, Conrad. All the time,' she said wretchedly.

'I don't believe this.' If the whole thing hadn't been so devastatingly horrible she might have found a glimmer of amusement in the astounded affront and scandalised resentment he was showing. 'I really don't believe what I'm hearing.'

'You told me you weren't capable of being close to anyone,' she continued softly, knowing she had to say it all. 'That love is a myth. That's what you said, Conrad. Well, I can't think like that. I could never give my body lightly. It would have to be a full commitment and I'd want the same promise of commitment back from the man I loved. It's the way I'm made.'

'And this man who let you down? Did he promise you full commitment and eternal devotion?' he challenged grimly.

Oh, he was good. He was; she had to give him that. She had noticed the raised eyebrow so she should have known something deadly was coming.

'No, he didn't,' she said bravely, her chin lifting proudly.

'And yet you still loved him.'

'It wasn't like that, not like you're assuming,' she said tightly, praying for courage. 'I never slept with David.'

'You didn't?' His eyes narrowed and she could almost see that razor-sharp mind whirring and collating all the facts so far. 'But since him you said—'

'That I've only dated occasionally, yes.' Perhaps it had to be this way for this ridiculous affair that wasn't an affair to finish, she thought painfully as humiliation turned her cheeks vivid scarlet. Conrad Quentin liked his women experienced and well-versed in the art of love, and although he had known she wasn't exactly a Mata Hari type he had thought—at twenty-six years of age—she had had some sexual experience.

The silence stretched and lengthened, but she was determined she wasn't going to break it, although the hand that reached out for her coffee cup was shaking. She had drained the last of the coffee before Conrad said, his voice expressionless, 'You should have told me, Sephy.'

'That I'm a virgin?' she stated baldly. The time for delicacy was over. 'Why? It's nothing to do with anyone else.'

'I'm not anyone,' he said sharply, before moderating his tone as he added, 'Hell, don't look like that.'

She couldn't help how she looked; he ought to be glad she hadn't dissolved into hysterical weeping the way she was feeling. Nevertheless, her chin went up a notch or two and she gripped her hands very tightly together under cover of the small pub table.

It had taken every drop of courage she possessed when she'd made the decision to leave her home town and move to London. The incident with David Bainbridge had shattered her self-confidence—which had always been pretty fragile anyway—and caused her to go into herself, but at the age of twenty she had known she had to climb out of the rut she'd made for herself and spread her wings.

The bedsit—which had been all she could afford—had been grotty to say the least, but she had persevered and worked hard and forced herself to go out on the occasional date so she didn't fall into the trap of becoming a recluse.

Her salary had risen nicely, she had found the flat of her dreams and a whole bunch of new friends, and then had come the chance of bolstering her career by standing in for Madge for a few weeks or—as it had turned out—months.

Every step along the way she had had to make herself reach out and be resolute in her determination that the episode with David would not spoil her life. From the start she had ignored the whispering and the nudges and sly looks as word had got about, and even though it had nearly killed her she had held her head high and refused to hide away, licking her wounds in private.

All that couldn't be for nothing, she told herself now. It was ironic that after all the years of keeping her feelings for the opposite sex in cold storage they had melted only for her to fall for the wrong man, but she would rise above this as she had risen above everything else. She loved him, she would always love him, but that was her problem, not his.

'So.' His eyes were still narrowed on her pale face. 'Where do we go from here?'

She took a deep breath, calling on the fortitude the silent pep-talk had given her, and said lightly, 'Back to London?'

'Don't be facetious, Sephy, it doesn't suit you,' he growled quietly.

'What do you expect me to do?' she snapped back swiftly, stung beyond measure. 'Dissolve into tears? String you along, knowing all the time it could never work?

Pretend? Coo and simper like your other women? That's not my style, Conrad.'

Her words fell into a taut silence, and then he completely took the wind out of her sails—and nearly sank her boat in the process—when he reached out and stroked his hand down the silky smooth skin of her cheek. 'You think I don't know that?' His voice was husky and smoky-soft. 'One thing I've come to know is that I always get the truth from you, even if it's like a punch in the stomach at times. And honesty deserves honesty. I can't give you what you deserve, Sephy, but I can't let go of you either. I *won't* let go of you.'

'That's so unfair,' she whispered weakly.

'Yes, it is,' he agreed quietly. 'So…how about if we get to know each other a while, without sex?'

'What?' The baldness of the last words had left her gasping.

'I respect you, Sephy, and I enjoy your company,' he said evenly, 'and I haven't said that to many women. But…I can't change the way I am. I don't believe in love and marriage and happy families and I won't insult you by saying there's a chance I might change. You say you couldn't accept anything less in a sexual relationship, so we cut the sex part.'

'But… I don't—' She was floundering; she had to pull herself together. 'Why?' she asked shakily. 'Why would you do that?' Knowing Conrad, there was a well-thought-out motive behind this.

'The only way I would want you in my bed is because you want to be there,' he said coolly. 'Regardless of what you think, I'm actually not an advocate of casual sex, neither have I ever enticed a woman with lies or my wealth or even the emotion of the moment. When eventually you come to me it will be knowing exactly what you are doing and because you have decided it is what you want too. And

I can promise you that as long as we are together I will be faithful. That's a darn sight more than most men commit to even when they are saying their marriage vows.' One dark raised eyebrow dared her to disagree.

'This…this is crazy.' And dangerous and scary and against every sensible and logical conclusion she had come to regarding Conrad Quentin. 'What if I say no?' she asked shakily.

'Then I'll make you change your mind,' he said softly, but with such cold purpose that her eyes opened wide.

'It will be for nothing; you say you can't change and neither can I,' she warned faintly. 'Not ever.'

'We'll see.' He smiled slowly and she felt her heart pound as the sky-blue eyes crinkled sexily. 'Not ever is a long, long time, and in the meantime we'll be having fun. There's nothing too terrible about that, is there?'

Sephy didn't know how to answer. She was aware, knowing Conrad as she now did, that he wasn't joking when he said he would determine to make her change her mind if she said no to this crazy scheme. It would make her a double challenge in his eyes, if nothing else.

And if she said yes? Her heart changed its rhythm into a mad gallop. It would mean a few weeks, maybe months, in his company with no strings attached. Memories. Memories that would have to last her a lifetime. And then when he at last accepted she wasn't going to sleep with him and they parted, he would at least remember her a little differently from all the rest. The one that got away? She bit on the soft underside of her bottom lip. And she would have to make sure she *did* get away.

But it was dangerous, too, too dangerous, loving him as she did. And she was the antithesis of his normal choice of female consort. How would she cope with his expectations of sparkling companionship? But then, she didn't have to.

She stared into the dark lean face wordlessly. The only way he would leave her alone would be when he lost interest. She didn't have to glitter and shine like all the society beauties he had been used to; she didn't have to worry that she didn't have an Armani or a Dior to her name and that she didn't know all the right people; she didn't have to try to be anything but herself. Sephy Vincent, with her old-fashioned views about love and marriage, her inexperience, her off-the-peg clothes and average good-looks.

The conclusion of this unlikely affair could only come one way; Conrad's tenacious, inflexible nature made it so. *He* had to end it because he didn't want her any more; she saw it clearly now. She just hoped she had the strength to endure it without giving him her body as well as her heart in the meantime.

'So, friends, then?' The smile she gave as she held out her hand was worthy of an Oscar if he did but know it.

'Not quite friends, Sephy, if you want that total honesty,' he said drily, his eyes hot as they roamed over her possessively. 'But I'll behave...for the time being. How about that?'

It was the best she was going to get, and far more than she could have hoped for that morning when the roses had arrived.

'It's a deal.'

And then, as he took her proffered hand and, instead of shaking it as she had expected, to seal the pact, raised it to his warm firm lips, the thought came that she had possibly just made the worst mistake of her life.

CHAPTER EIGHT

THE next few months were bittersweet. Sephy alternated between ecstasy and deep despair at regular intervals, sometimes on the same day, but in it all she sensed she was growing up fast and had left something of the old Sephy behind for ever. And that wasn't all bad.

It was impossible, as Conrad's 'companion', to avoid the glittering galas and functions his wealth and influence demanded he be at, and the first few times she accompanied him to a première or sat next to a famous personage at some dinner or other she felt totally out of her depth.

But then she discovered that even the most wealthy and well-known people were quite ordinary under their Guccis and sparkling diamonds, and that a ten-thousand-pound frock and jewellery from Cartier didn't necessarily make a lady.

At first Conrad tried to insist that she take a dress allowance from him for such occasions, but she objected so vehemently he had the good sense to desist. However, Sephy was aware that a man in his position couldn't have someone at his side who looked badly dressed, and here Maisie turned up trumps.

Under Maisie's rainbow-coloured hair was a brilliant clothes designer as well as an astute businesswoman, and when Sephy confided her predicament Maisie and her assistant got to work with their patterns and sewing machines.

The first dress, made just a week after she and Conrad had come to their arrangement, made Sephy's mouth fall open in sheer delight. 'Maisie, it's *gorgeous*,' she said as she tried on the sky-blue silk evening dress and watched what it did to her creamy skin and hair in Maisie's mirror. 'But how much do I owe you?'

'Nothing,' Maisie said offhandedly. 'I shall sell it in the shop when you've worn it. A woman in your position can't be seen wearing the same dress twice.' She grinned at Sephy, who smiled weakly back. 'You're a perfect size twelve so there won't be a problem; just don't spill red wine down it or something. And don't be shy about saying where you got it if any of the precious darlings ask, okay? Jenny and I will do something different for every do you go to—exclusives. Don't forget to mention they're exclusives.'

'Right.' Sephy looked at the vibrant, confident face in front of her and said, a touch regretfully, 'You'd be much better at all this than me, Maisie.'

'Possibly.' Maisie eyed her laughingly through her exotic eye make-up. 'But I'm not the one he's got the hots for, kiddo.'

Sephy gave an embarrassed laugh. 'He'll soon come to his senses,' she said quietly.

She had told Maisie the full story at the first fitting. It had been the first time she had shared how she felt about Conrad with a living soul and the relief had been tremendous. And Maisie had been tremendous too. She had listened without interrupting until Sephy had finished and then she had given her a big hug and muttered, 'He's a rat. A rich, sexy, drop-dead gorgeous rat, I admit, but a rat nevertheless. And he doesn't deserve you, sweetie.'

'He hasn't got me,' Sephy had answered with a wry smile.

'Just make sure you keep it that way!'

Part of keeping it that way was to follow through on her decision to leave Quentin Dynamics, which Sephy did at the end of February, when she joined a very elite and prestigious agency.

Conrad hadn't liked it when she'd told him she'd decided to join a temping agency for the foreseeable future, but she hadn't expected him to. Whilst she was still working for Mr Harper there was always the chance she would run into Conrad—in the lift, in Reception or one of the offices— and she didn't like the thought of that, now word had got out they were an item, but it was more the issue of independence that prompted her action.

She didn't feel comfortable in being reliant on Conrad for her bread and butter, and that was what working at Quentin Dynamics boiled down to. It didn't sit right. Also—and she found herself skirting over this thought even as she berated herself for not facing the inevitable—working somewhere else would make things much easier when their tenuous relationship was over.

And so she worked for the agency in the day and entered a different world at night; Conrad's world. A breathlessly exciting, fast-moving, exhilarating place where anything could—and frequently did—happen.

She found herself drawn into all aspects of his life, but during the times when she began to hope that Conrad cared for her more than he was prepared to admit she had to remind herself that her presence was still carefully controlled by that cool, analytical mind. She was aware he allowed her to get only so close, and then a remoteness, a very distinct withdrawal, would take place.

This happened more often after they had spent time together and it was just the two of them; quiet evenings at Conrad's beautiful home, long walks when they talked and laughed together, the odd meal at a little pub somewhere far away from the glitzy glamour restaurants Conrad normally frequented. If she was honest Sephy enjoyed these simple pleasures more than anything else, and as she had never been very good at hiding her feelings she suspected Conrad knew that. But he didn't know the underlying cause, that it was because she loved him and treasured the time alone when she had him all to herself.

Through the months leading up to the summer Conrad kept to his word. He kissed her often—he'd made it very plain in the first week of their new arrangement that he considered that perfectly permissible under the terms of their agreement—and he kissed her passionately, petting and cuddling her, but only up to a point.

He would fit her body into his when they sat watching TV at his home, his arm round her shoulders and his square chin resting on the silk of her hair so the delicious scent and warmth of him was all around her; draw her closely against him on their walks, his hard thigh nudging hers and the powerful height and breadth of him seeming to enclose her; hold her so close on the dance floor that she could feel every hard male inch of him. But always that restraint was there.

He was controlled and in command of himself at all times, coolly curbing his desire when he caressed or kissed her and checking any moments which had the potential to get out of hand.

Cool, calm and collected—the epitome of the composed, successful, imperturbable potentate. *And it was driving her bananas.*

How many times she'd felt an almost irresistible urge to just leap on him Sephy didn't know, but by the beginning of June it ran into the hundreds and it was sending her mad. *He* was sending her mad. Her nerves were frayed and she barely knew herself any more.

He was playing with her; they both knew it. Beneath the innocent guise of friendship, or whatever else he cared to label their strange relationship in the icy confines of that freezer which passed as a mind, he was playing a strategic game of emotional chess. He was sensual and sexy in a million provoking little ways, drawing forth a response from her body, inflaming her senses, rousing her and stimulating her libido until she didn't know what to do with herself, Sephy told herself bitterly as she sat picking at a slice of toast one morning after a terrible night's sleep.

Conrad had taken her to the theatre the evening before for the opening night of a play which was predicted to take London by storm. They had been invited to the champagne supper afterwards where they had met the cast before dancing the night away. And Conrad had been at his most devastating.

It hadn't just been the black dinner jacket and tie, although the formal attire suited his wicked dark looks to perfection, or the fact that he had towered head and shoulders above most of the other men present which had had her heart racing most of the night, but the way he had been with her.

Protective, proud, tender, attentive... He'd had the technique down to a fine art, as normal, she thought aggressively, jabbing marmalade on to an unfortunate piece of toast with enough force to reduce it to a pile of crumbs. No one watching them would have doubted that he was anything but madly in love with her.

She'd floated through the night, revelling in every magical second she'd spent in his arms, and then—just as they'd been thinking about leaving—another couple had come to their table to talk to them for a few moments.

The woman had been bubbly and flirtatious, with cute blonde curls and the biggest baby-blue eyes Sephy had ever seen, and her husband had been a tall, lean Richard Gere type, who'd clearly worshipped the ground his taffeta-clad wife walked on. They had made a striking couple, and had apparently only got married the month before, but from the first moment the other woman had looked at her Sephy had known the blonde had been one of Conrad's affairs and, moreover, that she still cared about him.

The knowledge had shocked her out of the state of euphoria the evening in his arms had produced and back into the real world with a bump.

'Who is she?' All the time the couple had been with them Sephy had promised herself she wouldn't ask, but the minute they were alone again the words had just popped out of their own accord.

Conrad didn't try to prevaricate after he saw the awareness in her face, but there was a cool, cutting note to his voice when he said, 'It was a long time ago, Sephy.'

'She still wants you.'

'They only got married four weeks ago, for crying out loud; they're still in the first flush of married bliss,' he said with a cynical, mocking smile. 'And Brian's rich enough to satisfy her.'

'She still wants you,' she repeated flatly.

The sapphire eyes narrowed and hardened, and then he shrugged off-handedly, his face taking on the sardonic, derisive expression Sephy hated. 'So?'

'Don't you *care*?' she asked painfully. This woman and Conrad had shared total intimacy, explored each other's bodies, probably done all sorts of things that she only dared to think about in the quiet darkness of her bed at night, and he could be so stone-cold about her. She didn't understand him; she really didn't.

'I told you, it was over a long time ago.' It was dismissive and curt and told her the conversation was over, but she couldn't leave it alone. She knew she ought to, and that the only person she was going to hurt was herself, but nevertheless she had to ask—even if she didn't really want to hear the answers.

'And you finished it, right?' She stared at him bravely.

The downward quirk to his bottom lip told her she was venturing on to thin ice but she found she didn't care. 'Didn't you?' she pressed tightly. 'You finished with her?'

'Yes, I did.'

'And you finish all your affairs.' It was a statement, not a question. 'The second anyone might get close or try to break out of the mould you deem acceptable, you terminate the liaison.'

He shrugged again. 'Don't waste any time feeling sorry for Katie, if that's how it is,' he said scornfully. 'The main thing she wanted in life was a generous meal ticket and that's what she's got. She was determined to live well, whatever it took.'

Sephy stared at him, her mind whirling with a hundred things she wanted to say but which suddenly seemed pointless in the face of his cold indifference.

The taxi ride home had been difficult and the conversation stilted—on her part at least—and she had barely slept all night. Her head was thumping now, and she felt weary and drained, but for the first time for months she was listening to what her subconscious had been trying to tell her all along.

There had been a part of her, a tiny core in her innermost being, that had hoped... Hoped he would mellow, that he would start to open up a little, that he would fall in love with her despite the bad odds. *Fool!* She slumped back in the chair, her eyes staring blankly straight ahead without seeing anything. She had been lying to herself all through this fiasco. Conrad wouldn't just give up and get tired of the chase; he wasn't like that. He was a hunter; she'd seen him in operation in the cut-throat world of business too often not to know that. And he always had to win.

The only way he would finish their liaison would be after she had become his and the chase was over, and if that happened she would never recover from the pain of it. If she gave herself to him it would be completely and for ever; he would drain her of everything she needed for the future, everything she had to give, and leave her empty and crushed and useless. She couldn't, she *wouldn't*, let that happen. This was self-preservation in its rawest terms.

At first she was too lost in her misery for the sound of the buzzer to register, and then, as it penetrated the blackness of her thoughts, she dragged herself up from the chair and walked into the hall. Conrad often sent her flowers at the weekend; no doubt it was a delivery.

'Yes?' Her voice was flat as she spoke into the intercom. Then, as a deep, husky voice said, 'Sephy?', her heart started pounding before she warned herself to take control.

'Conrad? What are you doing here?' He was due to pick her up later that afternoon for an evening barbecue with some friends of his who lived in Windsor, and she had been meaning to use the day to pretty herself up. Her hair needed washing, the flat was a mess—why was he here *now*? And then, as the panic subsided, she thought numbly perhaps this was for the best, after what the night before had shown her. Maybe it was better like this.

She could let this farce limp on for another few days or weeks or she could finish it now, and suddenly the second option was the only bearable one. He was never going to change; life with Conrad would be a savage cycle of highs and lows until the final low. And one day, when it was long over, he might catch a glimpse of her somewhere or other and his beautiful blue eyes would be as empty and cold as they'd been when he'd looked at Katie last night.

The last months had been nothing but moves on a chessboard to him, a means to an end, and it hadn't even seemed as though he had had much of a struggle to keep his hands off her.

She heard him say, a touch of amusement in his voice, 'I'm here to see you, of course,' and then she pressed the buzzer, indicating for him to come up, but she just couldn't speak.

'What's the matter?' The second he walked into the flat,

his arms full of flowers, his eyes focused on her ashen face. 'Are you unwell?' he asked quietly, his voice concerned.

She was dying. It was melodramatic, but exactly how she felt, and she wondered what his reaction would be if she said it out loud. As it happened she was beginning to feel a bit dizzy, and odder by the minute, but she merely said, 'I have to talk to you.'

His eyebrows rose enquiringly even as the blue gaze wandered down the length of her. She had the flimsiest of summer nighties on under her robe, but she blessed the fact the robe was thick towelling and covered her down to her knees as she pulled the belt tighter. Nevertheless her cheeks were burning.

'Tousled and barefoot. It suits you,' he said huskily as he dropped the flowers on to an occasional table and came towards her. 'You'd be nice to wake up next to in the morning, Sephy Vincent.'

If she was stupid, really stupid, she could believe that look in his eyes meant something, she told herself bleakly. But last night had solidified all her buried doubts and fears and this was truth time. 'For how long, Conrad?' she asked quietly.

'What?' She had caught him off guard and he stopped just in front of her, his arms freezing for a second as they reached for her waist and then continuing until he was holding her just a few inches from his hard chest. 'What do you mean?'

'I said for how long?' she repeated with a calm born of the numbness that had taken her over. 'How long would I be around?'

He was dressed in a suit and tie rather than casual clothes, which meant he was probably going into work for a few hours, and he confirmed this in the next moment when he said, his eyes slightly puzzled as they stared into hers, 'Look, I can't really stop now, there's some sort of crisis I need to sort out in the office for an hour or two, but I just wanted to give you the flowers and say I'll pick you up at three this afternoon, okay?'

'No, it's not okay. I'm sorry, Conrad, but I can't do this any more.' His hands were firm and warm through the towelling and he was as impeccably groomed as always, whereas she must look as though she had been dragged through a hedge backwards. It somehow seemed to sum up their relationship.

'You can't do what any more?' His voice was quiet, lazy even, but she had seen the import of her words register for a second in the intent blue gaze, and she knew he understood what she was saying. And he didn't like it; she knew that too.

'This, us, being together and not being together. Seeing that woman last night—' She stopped abruptly. She didn't know how to put it. 'I don't want to end up like her,' she said tightly.

'What?' He let go of her abruptly, stepping back a pace.

Her heart was thudding so loudly now it was echoing in her ears, but at least she could think better without him holding her, and the distance between them helped her to say fairly coherently, 'That's what you're trying to do, turn me into someone like her.'

'The hell I am!' He glared at her, his mouth pulling into a thin line as he said coldly, 'It might have slipped your memory, but this charade of being together and not being together was very much your idea, not mine, so don't try that little tack, Sephy. I don't know what meeting Katie has to do with anything—damn it, I haven't seen the woman in a couple of years—but if anyone should be griping it's me, not you. You've had this all your own way.'

'How can you say that?' Anger had flooded in, melting the numbness and bringing a rush of adrenalin that brought her ramrod-straight in front of him. 'How can you *dare* say that? I told you at the beginning I didn't want an affair with you—'

'And we both knew you were lying,' he said insolently, moving a pace nearer and staring down at her with glittering blue eyes. 'You want me, Sephy, and it's nothing to be ashamed about, for crying out loud! And you're not the only one who's had enough of this damn travesty. I've waited for you to come to your senses—longer than I've ever waited for any woman, I might add.'

'What do you expect me to say? Thank you?' she spat sarcastically, the pain in her heart enabling her to fight back.

'No, you can show your appreciation for my patience another way,' he said with hateful mockery.

'Not in a month of Sundays!' she shot back furiously, hiding the sudden dart of fear under her blazing rage.

'A month of Sundays?' He was towering over her now, and as he reached out and jerked her against him he said softly, 'I wouldn't have to wait two minutes, let alone a month of Sundays, and you know it. Tell me. Tell me you don't want me and I'll leave right now. Tell me to get out of your life, Sephy.'

'I—I don't want you,' she stammered. 'I want you to go.'

'Little liar.' He smiled, but it was a mere predatory twisting of his lips a second before they claimed her mouth.

'Let go of me!'

As she jerked her head away and struggled in his arms he made a low sound of irritation in his throat before renewing his assault on her senses, moulding her closer against his hard body.

If he had been rough or violent, if he had hurt her, she could have fought him and kept fighting, but his attack was warm and thrilling and frighteningly perceptive. She could feel his heart slamming against the hard wall of his chest and her own was an echo, her mouth opening under the continued assault and her head falling back against the sinewy strength of his arm.

The feel of him, the warmth and scent of his body, was wildly intoxicating, and as his hot hungry mouth trailed fire over her ears and throat before returning to take her mouth with gentle ferocity she knew the restraint he had been employing over the last months was all used up. He was going for the kill.

He was whispering her name, touching her and caressing her until her body was trembling, and she was moaning softly in her throat without being aware of it as she strained closer to him.

It was only when she felt cooler air on her hot flesh that she realised the robe was on the floor and she was only clothed in the dubious covering of the wafer-thin nightie, which exposed more than it concealed. It should have mattered but it didn't.

His hands were on the soft swell of her breasts, their peaks hard and urgent against his knowing fingers, before they moved to her slender waist and womanly hips, and as he fitted her soft feminine curves against the hard thrust of his arousal she could feel the alien raw power of his manhood through their clothes.

'Say you want me, Sephy, say it,' he muttered hoarsely against her lips, and as she opened her dazed eyes she looked into his and they were hot and midnight-blue. The cool façade had been well and truly blown apart—this was a man intent on possession. 'Tell me I'm right.'

What was she doing? As she stared into his face the thought hammered in her head. This was about more than proving one of them right, didn't he understand at least that? But, no, he didn't. If he could fit her into a nice convenient slot in his mind that was all he needed. But she didn't fit like the others, she just *couldn't* think and feel like them—she wanted all of him, not a taste now and again until even that was taken away.

'I do want you.' She knew exactly what she was doing as she spoke the next words that would provide the ultimate wedge between them. 'But it's because I love you. And not because of the sexual chemistry between us or your wealth or your looks or anything else that could be taken away or lost with fate or time. I love *you*, all of you, the complete man—warts and pimples and all. If you lost all your money tomorrow or were hurt or injured nothing would change in my feeling for you.'

'No.' One small word but it had the power to make her feel as though she was nothing. The look on his face, the stark disbelief and rejection was all she had feared and more. 'You're mistaking something very natural, the sexual chemistry you spoke of, for something that doesn't exist. You'll come to realise that in time, believe me.'

His hands had moved to her upper arms now and he was holding her slightly apart from him as he stared into her drowning eyes. 'If you had known other men you'd understand—'

'I don't want to know other men, Conrad.' She suddenly felt so weary, so drained, that even standing was an act of will. They were at opposite ends of the world, of the universe—there was no meeting point; there never had been. He wanted someone who was content with material things, someone he could buy, a woman who wouldn't make the mistake of caring. And right at this moment she felt that was what he deserved.

'You will,' he said tautly. 'In time you will.'

And then she understood. His childhood and youth, bad as they had been, weren't all of it. And unknowingly she repeated the essence of the words he had said to her months before. 'Who was she?' She should have known there was something—*someone*.

He let go of her, walking across to stand with his back to her as he stared out of the window into the sunny street below. As she struggled into her robe, shaking from head to foot, he said expressionlessly, 'She was just a female like any other, but I was young and idealistic and thought there was such a thing as love in those days. I was seventeen years old and she was the new French mistress at the school. Funny, eh? Like one of those bawdy jokes that make people laugh?'

He turned to face her then, and his countenance was dark and stony. 'Knowing what I know now, she must have been around some to get the experience she had, but she didn't look her age—she was twenty-six—and she lied so beautifully she could have made the devil himself believe black was white. She was tiny, petite, and she made every lad in the school feel like Tarzan, so the fact that she was sleeping with me... We were going to get married, as soon as I'd finished my A Levels and was out of that place. And then some weeks into the summer holidays, when I was waiting for my results and for her to join me after she'd settled things in France, I got a letter.'

A 'Dear John', Sephy thought painfully. She swallowed once, twice, before she managed to say, 'I'm sorry, I'm so sorry.'

'She'd married the local big-wig in her hometown,' Conrad said evenly. 'Apparently she'd been engaged to him for years but he was twenty-five years older than her and a gangster type with plenty of women on the side. She'd caught him out a few times and come to England in a fit of pique. Anyway, true love triumphed, or in her case a mansion of a house and her own Ferrari etcetera, etcetera, etcetera. A seedy little story involving seedy little people.'

'And that's when you went abroad,' she said softly, sinking down on to the sofa before her legs gave out. She felt sick for him, heartsick, but her misery was all the more acute for knowing that this was the death knell on any faint hope she'd had that he would ever understand how she loved him. He might want her, he might even care about her in his own way, but the ability for anything more had been burnt out of his soul long before he had met her. She had met him far, far too late.

Her head was swimming now, and she felt nauseous, but she forced herself to sit quietly. She sensed he had never spoken of all this before and he might never again, and she had to hear it all. She had to *know*.

'Yes, I went abroad,' he agreed expressionlessly. 'The original angry young man with money in his pocket and no one to answer to. I made a few mistakes—hell, I made a lot of mistakes—but it was beneficial in the main. I grew up, learnt what my strengths and weaknesses were and I found I was more like my parents than I cared to admit. I didn't need anyone to make good.'

'Everyone needs someone, Conrad,' she said sadly.

'That's where you're wrong, Sephy,' he said with disturbing conviction. 'Society perpetuates the myth that we're pack animals because it makes it easier for governments to control the hordes, that's all. Marriage, family units—they aren't necessary, believe me. I'm living proof of that.'

If she hadn't been so tired and her head hadn't been pounding so badly she might have thought more about what she said, but as it was the words were out before she had time to consider how they sounded. 'That's such rubbish,' she said flatly. 'Such utter and absolute rubbish. It's the most natural thing in the world for two people to fall in love and want to create a family. When it goes wrong it can be the most devastating thing in the world, like in your case, but that doesn't mean it's not necessary. If anything I would say you are living proof *for* a secure family unit rather than against. Proof of what a mess someone can become when they aren't loved and cherished by the very people they have a right to expect it from.'

He stared at her for a moment, the slash of colour along his chiselled cheekbones deepening as her words hovered in the taut silence. 'Thank you so much for that vote of confidence,' he said coldly, the tone of his voice cutting, 'but I don't think I've done too badly on the whole.'

'Materially you've got the world at your feet,' she agreed quietly, 'but that's nothing. Money and possessions are nothing.'

'There are a good number of women out there who would disagree with you.' It was bitterly cynical.

'Yes, there are.' This was it; this was the end. She had offended him beyond the point of no return. It was there in the blazing blue eyes and savagely tense jaw; he looked as though he would like to strangle her with his bare hands. 'And they are as emotionally crippled as you,' she said softly. 'No good to themselves and no good to anyone else. Life is more than performing well in bed, Conrad, more than making people fear and tremble when you walk into a room to conduct a business deal.'

'Here endeth the first lesson?' The sarcasm was raw and deadly. 'What makes you such an authority on human relationships anyway?' he said with biting control.

'I'm not an authority; I've never pretended to be,' she shot back tightly. 'But I know what I know and you're wrong, so wrong.'

'Oh, to hell with this,' he ground out furiously. 'I've a deal worth millions hanging in the balance. That's real life! And if I can have a few of them in fear and trembling this morning that'll suit me just fine; it'll have been a successful day.'

'Then I feel sorry for you,' she said bravely, lifting her chin as she stared up at him from the sofa. 'If that's all you've got.'

'Keep your pity for someone who needs it, Sephy,' he said with sudden chilling softness. 'Because I don't.'

'No, of course, I'd forgotten.' She was so *angry* with him; he would never find anyone else who would love him as she did and he was throwing away her chance of happiness along with his. This was so *unfair*. 'You don't need anyone, do you?'

'Dead right.'

She knew he was going to walk out on her and she steeled herself not to move or speak as he left, nodding at him with almost clinical detachment as he turned in the doorway to survey her one last time. The look on his face chilled her to the bone.

And then the door closed behind him, she heard his feet on the stairs outside—a brief pause—and then the sound of the door into the street being slammed with some force. He had gone. She turned her face into the upholstered plumpness of the sofa and let the pent-up tears come in an overwhelming flood. She had known it was going to happen—that it *must*. There had only been one way this could all finish from the start, so why—knowing that—did it still hurt so much?

It was a good half an hour later before Sephy roused herself from the sofa, and by then she had realised—her desolation taken as read—that she wasn't feeling physically well.

Her throat was burning, there were a hundred little men with hammers inside her head and she felt as exhausted as if she had just completed the London Marathon.

In spite of her consuming misery she fell asleep immediately she crawled back into bed, and it was some time later—how long she had no idea—that she became aware of Maisie's voice talking to her as a soft hand shook her awake. 'Sephy, Sephy, are you all right? For goodness' sake talk to me, kiddo. What's wrong?'

'Wh-what's the matter?' she asked groggily, the urgent, almost tearful note in Maisie's voice penetrating the consuming heaviness as she struggled to open her eyes.

'I've been pressing the buzzer for ages, and then I tried ringing; we were supposed to meet for coffee and croissants this morning, remember?' Maisie said earnestly. 'So I got the pass key from Jerry; he's waiting in the living room.'

'Is he?' She tried to sit up but every bone was aching and she felt indescribably ill. It was easier to fall back against the pillows.

'You've got a fever. I'm calling the doctor,' Maisie said firmly.

She heard Maisie speak, but it was too much effort to answer, and it was the same through the doctor's visit. She was aware of people in the room, but it was as though they were at the end of a long foggy corridor, and although she struggled to answer the questions put to her she wasn't at all sure she was making sense.

'Shouldn't be left alone...' The odd few words filtered through the pounding in her head. '...need me, don't hesitate to call.' She tried to sit up and protest that she would be perfectly all right if only everyone would *go*, but the room started to revolve into a spinning kaleidoscope of colour and sound that took the last of her strength with it.

The next twenty-four hours passed in a blur of images and weird disjointed dreams. She thought she heard Conrad's voice at one point, and then Maisie, if not exactly shouting, then coming pretty near to it. She was conscious of trying to claw her way out of a deep abyss, but every time she thought she was going to make it it all got too much, and the world became narrowed down to a thick heavy blanket that drew her down and down...

When she did finally awake properly she lay for some moments without opening her eyes, aware that the terrifying headache was gone, along with the swirling voices and distorted images which had populated her head. She felt tired, she didn't think she had ever felt so tired in all her life, but her mind was her own again.

She forced her aching eyelids open, and then blinked and shut them again as golden sunlight turned everything white for a moment.

'Sephy? Sephy, it's Maisie. Open your eyes again, love.'

Maisie? As her gaze focused on her friend's face Sephy saw to her consternation that Maisie looked as tired as she felt. 'What...what are you doing here?' she asked through dry lips.

'Looking after you,' was the rueful reply. 'You've been on planet Zargos for the last twenty-four hours, kiddo. Don't you remember?'

'A bit.' And then, as her thirst became overwhelming, 'Can I have a drink, Maisie?' But by the time the glass was placed to her dry lips she was fast asleep again.

By Sunday evening Sephy had skimmed in and out of sleep several times, but was sufficiently recovered to sit up in bed and drink the bowl of steaming vegetable soup Maisie gave her at six o'clock. She didn't feel at all hungry but she tried to please Maisie.

'You had us going for a time there, kiddo,' Maisie said breezily as she plumped herself down on the duvet. 'The doctor thought it was this rotten summer flu, but I was beginning to doubt he knew what he was talking about. He said you're absolutely knackered as well, which didn't help. Asked me if you'd been burning the candle at both ends,' she added pointedly.

'And you said?'

'Too right.' Maisie grinned cheerfully. 'I told him you'd got this rat of a boyfriend who'd been giving you the run-around.'

'You didn't!' Sephy was horrified. 'You didn't, Maisie?'

'I did.' Maisie's kohl-blackened eyes narrowed. 'And I

told the boyfriend the same thing, as it happens. He didn't take too kindly to being told he was a git,' she said with some satisfaction.

'Maisie!' The soup nearly went all over the bed.

'Now don't excite yourself,' Maisie said imperturbably. 'It won't do him any harm in the long run.'

'He...Conrad came round here?' Sephy asked weakly. She had purposely been blanking that part of her consciousness until she felt strong enough to deal with the memory of their last meeting.

Maisie nodded. 'I think he wished he hadn't by the time he left,' she said with some relish, the stud in her nose shining as she wrinkled her nose gleefully at the memory.

'Oh, Maisie.' She felt too weak to deal with this development.

'Don't "Oh, Maisie" me,' the other girl said firmly. 'From what you mumbled when you were delirious, I got the impression he'd chucked you. Right?'

Sephy nodded silently. Words were beyond her just at this point, with the picture of an angry, bristling Maisie facing the tall, remote figure of Conrad Quentin and giving him what for. She was one in a million; she was really.

'Yes, that's what I thought,' Maisie said comfortably. 'So I told him he ought to be down on his knees thanking God or Buddha or whoever else he prays to that they threw you across his path. You're special, Sephy.' Now all trace of belligerence was gone as Maisie leant forward and gripped her hand hard. 'Very special, and he's a fool. I told him that as well.'

'Oh, Maisie.' She didn't seem able to say much else, but the other girl's fierce championship was making her want to cry. She had never been one to make close friends in the past, her inferiority complex as a child and adolescent had worked against her in that respect, but now she realised there was a whole realm of warmth and friendship open to her she had never guessed at.

'Anyway, that's enough of that.' Maisie jumped to her feet, her psychedelic hair, bright green waist-length cardigan and tight rainbow-coloured skirt all—miraculously—blending into one very attractive whole as she said, 'You've wasted enough tears on that rat; you're not going to shed another one. You've finished the soup and now you're going to eat a chicken sandwich prepared by my own fair hand. Okay, kiddo?'

'Okay.' Sephy nodded obediently.

She only managed to eat about a third of the chicken sandwich before she found herself snuggling down in bed again and falling asleep, but an hour later when the buzzer went she was wide awake in an instant, as though she had been programmed.

She could hear Maisie speaking in a low voice into the intercom, although she couldn't distinguish what was being said, but when the other girl popped her head round the bedroom door a few moments later Sephy was sitting up in bed with her eyes fixed on the door. 'I heard the buzzer. Who is it?' she asked nervously.

'He wants to come up for a few minutes.' Maisie's voice was flat and low and Sephy didn't have to ask who 'he' was.

To her eternal shame Sephy was less concerned with the ethics of it all than the fact that she hadn't bathed in forty-eight hours and her hair was tangled and she must look a sight. 'No.' She stared at Maisie and the bizarrely painted face stared back. 'Not now. Say…say I'm still too ill or something.'

'Sure.' She certainly wasn't going to get any argument from Maisie. 'Let the creep squirm for a while.'

She didn't want him to squirm. Ridiculous in the circumstances, but she really didn't want him to squirm, Sephy thought miserably, as she slid down under the duvet again.

It was a few minutes before Maisie walked back into the bedroom, and this time she was carrying a huge bunch of flowers and a box of chocolates that outdid the colossal absurdity Conrad had taken in to Madge. 'Okay, so he's a generous creep,' Maisie said offhandedly before grinning at her and adding, 'I told him to come back tomorrow, but that's about as far as I can push my luck, I think. As it is he's phoned the doctor himself and got the lowdown on what's happening. Dead cheek if you ask me.'

'He didn't?' And then she refused the ray of hope before it had a chance to develop into something more hurtful. He was probably only feeling a bit guilty, she told herself silently. As well he might! But it didn't make any difference to the overall situation and she'd forget that at her peril. 'How did he know my doctor?' she thought out loud. 'I've never told him.'

'Probably from his personnel department,' the ever practical Maisie said in reply. 'You did work for him for six years, remember.'

As if she could ever forget!

Sephy insisted on sending Maisie back to her own flat to get a good night's sleep, but after the other girl had gone the hot bath and long soak she'd promised herself degenerated into a hasty lick and a promise followed by brushing her teeth. She couldn't believe how exhausted she felt once she'd tottered into the bathroom, and by the time she slid back under the rumpled covers her legs were shaking and her eyelids just wouldn't stay open.

The next morning she awoke very early and lay looking at the vases of flowers—the bouquet wouldn't fit into less than two—sitting on her dressing table. The freesias and stock had scented the room with summer, and red and gold chrysanthemums and coneflowers were a blaze of colour against the graceful belladonna lilies standing at the back of the profusion of flowers.

Maisie had already told her that the blooms Conrad had previously bought on the Saturday morning were filling the sitting room's large windowsill, and for a moment—just a moment—Sephy found herself resenting the inoffensive flowers.

It was too easy to send bouquets and buy chocolates and other expensive presents, she told herself wearily. They only cost him money, and for someone as rich as Conrad money wasn't a consideration. A fistful of garden daisies or buttercups given with love would have sent her to the moon, but he wouldn't understand that, or even perhaps believe it. And that wrenched her heart.

She had often looked at film stars or top models in the past who had all but destroyed themselves in some way— drink, drugs, depression leading to attempted suicide—and wondered how they could fall apart when they had the world at their feet and everything they wanted, but even the best things counted as nothing if you didn't have your soulmate to share them with.

But Conrad wasn't her soulmate, however much she wished it different. She couldn't turn him into something he wasn't any more than he could make her give up the loving, giving part of herself that made her what she was, the part which would become an irritation to him—at best—if she put both feet into his world.

He wanted a cool, worldly Caroline de Menthe clone and she needed roses round the door and happy ever after, something he just wasn't capable of providing.

Maisie breezed in just before eight and insisted on cook- ing her fried eggs and bacon with two rounds of toast be- fore she disappeared to the boutique, with promises she would return at lunchtime with sandwiches. 'Don't you dare try and do a thing today,' she warned firmly as she placed the loaded tray across Sephy's knees. 'The doctor said a week in bed at least.'

'Maisie, I hate staying in bed!'

'Well, you can get up and lie in the sitting room,' the other girl conceded, 'but that's all. Have a bath, drift around looking pale and interesting and prepare to twist the knife when he - who - deserves - his - comeuppance calls. Okay, sweetie?'

'Maisie, you're the most unlikely mother hen in the whole of creation.' Sephy grinned with genuine warmth.

'I know it.' There was a vivid shade of purple coating Maisie's eyelids today which exactly matched her mini-dress, and as the other girl winked at her Sephy laughed out loud. As desolate as she was feeling about Conrad, there was something irrepressible about Maisie that lifted one's spirits in spite of oneself.

Once she was alone Sephy forced down a few mouthfuls of food and then slept most of the morning, before rising just after eleven and running herself the promised bath. She had been feeling so warm and sticky that the silky water felt heavenly, and after soaking for some minutes she washed her hair, luxuriating in digging her fingers into her scalp and washing out the staleness of the weekend.

Once out of the bath she wrapped a big fluffy bath sheet round herself sarong-style, and peered into the mirror. A brief glance was enough to inform her that the pale and interesting look Maisie had mentioned was definitely in evidence, although she wasn't sure the interesting part applied.

Her face was lint-white, the sprinkling of freckles across her nose standing out like a scattering of nutmeg on thick cream, and she actually looked thinner. 'Every cloud has a silver lining,' she muttered wryly to herself as she walked through into the bedroom to dry her hair.

When the buzzer sounded she grimaced to herself and

then glanced at her little bedside alarm clock. Twelve o'clock—Maisie was nothing if not punctual.

She padded quickly through to the hall, surprised to find how much the bath had tired her, and flicked the switch on the intercom as she said, 'Come on up, mother hen. Your chick's just drying her hair,' before opening the flat's front door and walking through to the sunlit sitting room.

And it wasn't until she heard footsteps that definitely were not Maisie's that she realised Maisie would have used Jerry's key.

CHAPTER NINE

THERE was no time to think, let alone move, and as the tall, lean figure of Conrad walked into the flat Sephy faced him from the middle of the sitting room, her hair falling in thick, damp, rich brown waves about her pale face and bare shoulders, and her honey-gold eyes open wide with shock.

He stopped still in the doorway as he saw her, and in spite of herself she let her eyes feast on him for a moment; she really couldn't help it. His hard, handsome face was full of very sharply defined planes and angles as a shaft of sunlight hit him, and his coal-black hair and impossibly blue eyes, the tailor-made suit and silk shirt and tie, completed the picture of a man who knew exactly where he was going and woe betide anyone who got in his way on the journey. A man at the top of his profession.

Cold, hard and ruthless; he could definitely be called that on occasion, and yet she had seen the other side of the coin, and it was that which made her heart ache and her senses tighten to breaking point. And it was that weakness she had to fight now.

She had never felt so vulnerable and defenceless, and something of what she was feeling must have shown in her face because he said, his voice soft and steady, 'It's all right, Sephy. I'm not here to fight.'

'I...I thought you were Maisie,' she murmured breathlessly.

'Ah, the coffee and croissants, right?'

It was the smile that did it.

He could smile. He could actually *smile* like that, as though nothing was wrong, when he had all but ripped her

165

heart out by its roots in this very room not three days ago, Sephy thought bitterly. But at least his casual demeanour had the effect of putting adrenalin in her veins and steel in her backbone.

He probably expected her to beg and plead or cry buckets, but she'd rather be hung, drawn and quartered! Pride and dignity were poor bedfellows but they were all that was left to her, and by golly she intended to hang on to them.

In the past she had always tried to make things easy between them by filling in any awkward silences with chatter, but now she lifted her head slightly and continued to stare at him without speaking. She was blowed if she was going to speak next.

'How are you feeling?' he asked after a few endless seconds.

'I'm fine,' she said tightly.

'Rubbish. How are you feeling?'

Typical Conrad! Well, if he wanted the truth he could have it. 'Tired, my throat's sore, the headache I thought had gone is returning—' since you walked through the door '—and I ache all over. Okay?' she snapped testily. 'Satisfied?'

'You really are in a bad mood, aren't you?' he drawled lazily, and then, as she opened her mouth to fire back, he added, 'I'm sorry I didn't realise you were ill on Saturday, Sephy.'

She shrugged, and then as the towel slipped a little decided she wouldn't do that again. 'It wouldn't have made any difference. We had things to say and we said them,' she said shortly.

Why did he have to look so good in a suit and tie? Why did he have to look so good in *anything*? she asked herself silently.

'The doctor told me you are extremely run down and

could do with a break,' Conrad said quietly. 'All those months of working all hours for me started a downward spiral, no doubt.'

She had to get something on other than this towel! 'Look, I won't be a moment,' she said curtly, before walking quickly into the bedroom and shutting the door. She stood for a second, her heart thumping so hard it made her feel dizzy, and then pulled on a baggy T-shirt and a pair of panties before slipping into her robe and jerking the belt tight. Psychologically fortified, she opened the door and walked into the sitting room, saying, 'Conrad, why did you come back on Saturday? Maisie told me.'

'Ah, yes, Maisie.' He frowned, and then said with grudging generosity, 'She's a good friend.'

'Yes, she is.' And Maisie knew as well as she did that her present exhaustion was due to the fact she'd lived on her nerves from the first day she had worked for Conrad Quentin. And it had got worse, a million times worse, since she'd agreed to his preposterous demand that they see each other. And she also knew, as she stared at his dear face, that she could never go back to that, even if the pain of losing him continued to the day she died. She felt light-headed, and sank down quickly on the sofa as she said, 'Please go.'

His guilt she could do without, and it was clear pity was the only thing he felt for her. Not once since he had walked through the door had he made any attempt to touch her, and she found she couldn't bear it. She just couldn't bear it.

'Not yet.'

To her horror he walked across and knelt back on his heels in front of her, the pose stretching material tight over hard male thighs and bringing the scent and warmth of him too close for comfort. He was looking straight into her eyes now, his dark head on a level with hers and the blue of his eyes piercing.

His voice dropped an octave as he said, 'Do you trust me, Sephy?' The tone was cool and almost expressionless.

'What?' Of all the things she had expected him to say it wasn't this. 'What are you talking about?'

'I need to know about this man, this David.' His eyes watched his words sink in, and as hot colour stained her white face he leant a little closer, not touching her with any part of himself yet enveloping her with his magnetic pull. 'I've no right to ask—after Saturday I haven't even got the right to be here, as Maisie's pointed out more than once—but nevertheless...'

'I...I can't.' She took a deep breath and managed to say, 'We're not seeing each other any more so what's the point?'

'I need to know, Sephy,' he said softly, his eyes never leaving her face for a moment. 'Believe me, I really need to know.'

She expelled a shuddering breath as her stomach churned violently. She could see this meant a great deal, but she didn't understand why, and the humiliation and pain of having to tell was too much. And it wasn't fair to ask, not now.

'Please?' It was said very, very softly.

He had never said that word before, and he had never looked at her as he was doing now. She couldn't read what was in his eyes but it was clear he was in the grip of something that was tearing him apart. And in spite of everything she couldn't bear that.

Her profile was white and fragile as she turned slightly, her voice low and strained as she began. 'There were a whole bunch of us who grew up together and David was one of them. He...he was the handsome one, the charmed one; everyone was crazy about him and wanted to be with him. And then...'

It didn't take long to tell, but when she had finished she sagged against the sofa as though she had been talking for hours. She hadn't looked at him once as she had spoken, and he hadn't said a word, so when his voice came, dark and deadly, saying, 'I would like to kill him, Sephy,' she was actually shocked.

'It was a long time ago; it's in the past,' she said quickly, feeling it had been a terrible mistake to tell him.

'I'm going to hold you, just hold you.' He had taken her in his arms before she could demur, lifting her as he rose and then sitting on the sofa so that she was cradled in his arms with her head resting against his throat.

She held herself rigid—it was either that or turning in to him and saying she would take any terms, any conditions, as long as he didn't go. But it would be a mockery of a relationship. He didn't love her; *he didn't love her.*

'Listen to me for a minute without saying anything,' he said huskily, after what felt like a lifetime. 'You're ill now, tired and low and at the end of yourself, and I should have realised it weeks ago. The doctor said you are completely exhausted.'

'But—'

'No, just listen, Sephy. I want you to do one last thing for me. I want you to let me send you away somewhere hot and lazy, somewhere where you can recover in peace and quiet and get strong again. Will you let me do that, please? And soon?'

She swallowed once, twice, but she still couldn't speak. He was sending her away, that much had registered, along with the knowledge that for a moment—just a split second of a moment—she had hoped he was going to say something else. That he had grown to love her, that their quarrel on Saturday had opened his eyes and he understood he felt more for her than he'd felt for the others. Had there ever been such a fool as her in the whole of time? Would she never learn?

He was breathing hard, she could feel his muscled chest rising and falling, and then he cleared his throat and said, 'Will you let me do that? The doctor says you need to convalesce.'

Nothing more than a weak whisper could force its way past the painful constriction in her throat as she fought the tears. 'There's no need, really. I am strong, or I will be in a day or two. It's only a touch of flu.'

'You haven't had a holiday in over a year and you're physically and mentally exhausted. I want to do this, Sephy. I've a place in Italy that I bought years ago, when Daniella's father first made contact with me again. It was a means of being around my niece now and again but still having home comforts and being able to work when I needed to. There are people there who will cook and clean and take care of things while you relax and get well again.'

'You mean live in your home?' she asked dazedly.

'This is not a means of getting you into my bed whilst you're ill and weak,' he said evenly, his voice slightly clipped now. 'I don't operate like that.'

'I know.' She hadn't thought that for a moment. 'I know that.'

'I shan't be there, of course, but I'll know you're recovering in beautiful surroundings and that there are people to assist if you need anything. You have my word I won't visit or harass you.'

His duty—as he saw it—taken care of and this whole unlikely affair finished on a clean note. She knew what he was about, but with the warm fragrance of him all about her and his body touching hers she couldn't think clearly.

'I can't...let you do that,' she said after a while.

She heard him sigh impatiently and then her heart stopped beating as she felt his hand smooth back a tendril of hair from her cheek, and he said, 'Yes, you can. Madge has sung your praises more than once for the way you handled things when she was away, and she's let me know it was totally unreasonable of me to expect you to work the hours she does. You're young; your whole life isn't taken up with Quentin Dynamics like she's chosen for hers to be.'

No, her whole life was taken up with him, and that was a hundred times worse than the position Madge was in.

So... Madge had obviously been on at him, and Maisie had put in her twopenny-worth, and now he felt he had to do something for her. She didn't like that, it was humiliating, but, knowing Conrad as she did when he had the bit between his teeth, he wouldn't take no for an answer, and besides... She bit her lip hard as she faced the truth of it. She would love to see this other home of his, live somewhere that had the imprint of him all around, even if it was just for a week or so. It was crazy and smacked of masochism but it meant she didn't have to let go for just a bit longer, that she was still on the perimeter of his life in some way. She closed her eyes and drank in the closeness of him for a moment. And she couldn't feel worse than she was feeling now. At least this way she would start to face the rest of her life without him bronzed and well instead of pale and pathetic.

'Look on this as a bonus for the job you did for me,' the deep, husky voice above her head said softly, 'if that makes you feel better.'

It didn't. It only confirmed what she'd known all along—that he was making this offer because he felt uncomfortable about the way things had finished and wanted to end their relationship on a better note. However, once he had touched her, once he had shown that other side of himself which was so dangerously tender, her earlier resolution regarding pride and dignity seemed to have flown out of the window.

She sighed inwardly at her inconsistency, and at the fact that she would be quite content to sit here like this for the rest of her life, and took a deep, steadying breath before she said, 'You don't have to do this, but if you really want to then…thank you. A holiday would be nice.'

If he was surprised at her easy capitulation he didn't show it, but, never one to miss pressing an advantage, he said quickly, 'A month away should have you back on your feet.'

'A month!' She straightened then, twisting to face him, and wished she hadn't as his face came disturbingly close. For such an uncompromisingly masculine man he had ridiculously long eyelashes, and his mouth was fascinatingly uneven. And sexy. Definitely sexy. It made you want to kiss it, to draw his firm bottom lip between yours and explore its taste…

'Okay, you've twisted my arm. Six weeks.'

'I can't possibly stay away a month,' Sephy said flatly, pulling the belt of the robe tighter before she twisted and rose carefully to her feet. She noticed—with a dart of pain that was confirmation she'd been stark staring mad to agree to anything but a swift clean break with this man—that he made no effort to restrain her or pull her back into his arms. 'Ten days at most.'

'A month minimum,' he said coolly, 'and of course it goes without saying I pay your rent here while you're away.'

'No way.' This was the Conrad she could fight, the imperious, overbearing, lordly tycoon who thought he only had to speak and the world listened. '*I* pay the rent.'

'Okay, I'm willing to compromise. *You* pay the month's rent,' he agreed smoothly.

She stared at him uncertainly. Somehow she had agreed to a month's holiday and she wasn't quite sure how. 'Conrad—'

As they both heard the downstairs door open, followed by a 'Yoohoo! It's only me!' Conrad's eyebrows rose mockingly.

'Mother hen?' he murmured silkily as he rose to his feet.

How could you love someone and hate them at the same time? 'Conrad, we have to discuss this,' she said a trifle desperately.

'No time.' And then he had pulled her into him roughly, kissing her hard and hungrily for a heart-stopping moment before he let her go, a second before Maisie breezed into the room.

'Hallo, Maisie,' he said easily, the mocking expression intensifying as he took in the look of absolute amazement on Maisie's face. 'How nice to see you again.'

'You... How did you—'

'Sephy will explain,' he said smoothly. 'By the way, she's going away for a few weeks the day after tomorrow. Help her pack, there's a good girl, and a taxi will be here at eight on Wednesday morning.'

'Conrad, I need to know about everything,' Sephy said flusteredly, her face flushed and the feel of his mouth still burning her lips. 'I have to get plane tickets and—'

'All taken care of.' And as she started to protest his eyes narrowed and he said warningly, 'I told you, Sephy, I want to do this and I don't do things by half. You should know that by now. Madge will phone you tonight and give you all the details; all you have to do is to get well enough to travel on Wednesday. Your passport is up to date?' he asked suddenly, as the thought struck him.

'Yes, but—'

'Good.' He turned briefly to Maisie, who for once was speechless, her startlingly mauve eyes blinking helplessly and the plate of sandwiches she had brought in wobbling precariously in her limp hand. 'I'll see myself out,' he said with silky politeness. 'You take care of your…chick.'

And then he was gone, leaving the two girls staring at each other as the sound of his footsteps on the stairs outside faded into the street.

CHAPTER TEN

PARADISE. This was one place which was paradise on earth and she wished with all her heart she didn't have to leave it tomorrow.

Sephy stretched on the sun lounger and reached for her sunglasses before sitting up and looking out over the glittering blue water of Conrad's Olympic-size swimming pool.

She drew her knees up to her chest, wrapping her arms round them and feeling a dart of pleasure at the smooth, golden-brown intensity of her tan.

From the first day she had arrived in Northern Italy the weather had been wonderful, day after gloriously sunny day turning her golden brown and highlighting her hair with shades of chestnut and dark auburn, and now she was as brown as Daniella.

She had been surprised to find Conrad's niece waiting for her at the airport when she had emerged from a luxurious first-class plane ride; Madge had merely said she would be met by a member of Conrad's Italian family but that was all. However, it had emerged that Enrico's time at the London hotel was finished and Conrad was setting the couple up with their own restaurant in their hometown, much to the delight of Daniella, who had apparently been homesick for Italy.

And Sephy had soon been able to understand why. She hadn't realised that the country held such vast contrasts; golden, powdery beaches and azure seas, rolling hillsides and magnificent mountain ranges, enchanting valleys and rich meadows where swathed figures still herded animals with tiny bell necklaces, small picturesque villages which hadn't changed in hundreds of years and great modern bustling towns where it seemed as though every other car was a Ferrari—Daniella had shown her it all.

Conrad's villa, set high in wooded hills above the town where his relatives lived, was an old mansion he had had completely refurbished when he had decided to buy the dignified, crumbling, graceful old residence. And Sephy had fallen in love with it the moment she had seen it.

Mellow, honey-coloured old stone, arched leaded windows, exquisite wrought-iron balconies cascading with bougainvillaea of vibrant red and mauve, all topped by a rich terracotta-tiled roof—the house had it all. It was surrounded by beautifully landscaped gardens, sheltered by massive oak trees and cypress, and with the huge swimming pool and orchards at the back of the house the grounds were extensive.

An old Italian couple—distant relatives of Daniella's father—kept house for Conrad and resided in a large, spacious flat above the row of garages converted from the original stables, and a gardener and a cleaning lady who lived in the town visited on a daily basis.

Sephy had been amazed Conrad had never mentioned the villa in all the months she had known him, but when she had said as much to Daniella the Italian girl had shrugged extravagantly in true Latin style before saying, 'Conrad, he like to keep it separate, *si*? He very private man, very independent. This different.'

At Sephy's puzzled look, Daniella had continued, 'He never bring no one here from outside, from his other life. Not ever, *si*? This is where he is himself, I think.'

'He's brought me.'

'*Si.*' Daniella had looked at her oddly then, her nutbrown eyes slanting above finely moulded cheekbones. '*Si*, he bring you, Sephy.'

Sephy had wondered, at first, if Conrad would visit whilst she was staying, but as day had followed day and then week had followed week she'd realised he intended to keep to his word and remain in England. However, he'd made a point of phoning her every night at the same time without fail.

At first their phone conversations had been stilted and awkward, and had lasted no more than five minutes or so, but gradually they had lengthened into interesting, often laughter-filled discussions, and after two weeks it hadn't been unusual for the phone to be occupied for over an hour. And, perhaps predictably, Sephy had found she was measuring time from call to call and only really coming alive when she heard the deep, dark voice on the other end of the line.

Conrad had talked about all sorts of things he had never discussed before; his plans for the future regarding the Quentin empire, difficulties or triumphs he encountered day by day, even Angus's emergency trip to the vet, when the big cat had taken on a bunch of the local feline mafia and exited from the scrap minus part of his left ear.

'Of course he managed to bleed all over the car,' Conrad had said drily, 'and Madge was so upset I bought a bottle of brandy on the way home, not realising she'd never had spirits before. She was so out of it after two totties I had to sleep the night on her settee in case she fell down the stairs or something.'

The girls in the office at Quentin Dynamics would never have recognised the cold, unemotional, heartless tycoon and his dragon of a secretary, Sephy had thought with an inward chuckle. Which, for no reason at all that she could name, had suddenly turned into an overwhelming urge to have a good cry.

She had restrained herself until she was off the phone but then had bawled half the night. At three in the morning she had given herself a stiff talking-to, followed Madge's example of getting legless, and then slept like a top until two the next afternoon.

After that she had kept a firm hold on her emotions, both before, during and after the telephone calls, but it still hadn't stopped her *aching* to hear his voice.

'Which doesn't help anyone in the long run, old girl,' she told herself now, levering herself off the lounger and walking idly to the edge of the swimming pool. Tomorrow had to be cut-off point. Once she was back in England she had determined she'd move right away from London, probably up north, maybe even as far as Scotland. She could possibly think about moving abroad later too.

She had to make a new life for herself; she saw it now. Not back in her hometown—much as she loved her mother, that wouldn't work—but somewhere fresh and challenging. And far away from London.

She stood gazing down into the flickering water, immersed in sober thought. It was a baking hot, airless afternoon, and the sun was beating down fiercely on her skin now she had moved out of the shade the large parasol fixed over the sun lounger had provided, but still she didn't move.

Maisie had called him a rat, but she couldn't think of him like that. In his own way he had always been very honest with her. She wished she didn't love him. Her eyelids smarted and she told herself, Don't. Don't do this; it's pointless. Look forward. She wished she didn't keep dreaming about him, longing for the feel of his arms about her. She wished she knew for sure if she'd done the right thing in not taking what he could give for as long as he could give it so she'd got memories of waking up beside him, feeling him inside her, knowing the ecstasy of full intimacy.

'Sephy?'

She froze for a second before giving herself a little shake. She was imagining things now—all she needed. Nevertheless, something told her to turn round, and there he was. Not more than a few feet away.

She would have loved to be able to behave as he expected. Like a Caroline de Menthe would have behaved. But she couldn't. A glib, cool response was beyond her.

She stared at him, at the big, dark, *magnificent* sight of him, and she began to tremble. He looked calm and composed, impeccably dressed as always, in charcoal-grey trousers and a short-sleeved silk shirt in a lighter hue, and here she was in a minuscule denim bikini she had worn nonstop practically since arriving in Italy and which, she had noticed yesterday, was showing signs of wear in several strategic places.

'You look wonderful,' he said softly, taking another step towards her and then stopping as she instinctively jerked backwards, almost disappearing into the pool in the process.

'Conrad.' It was a faint murmur but all she could manage through the wild beating of her heart which was sending the blood tumbling through every nerve and sinew.

Pull yourself together. Funnily enough it was Maisie's voice she heard through the feverish rush of adrenalin and it worked to some extent, enabling her to take a long deep breath and say fairly coherently, 'I didn't know you were coming. No one said.'

'I told them not to.'

'Oh.' That look on his face was a lie; it wasn't real. She was imprinting what she wanted to be there, she told herself desperately. She hadn't learnt anything over the last weeks.

'Don't you want to know why?' he asked softly.

'I...I'm sure you must have had your reasons.'

'Oh, yes, I did.' He was watching her as though he couldn't take his eyes off her, and now, when he moved towards her, Sephy held still. 'I wanted to see if you still looked at me the way you did for an instant that afternoon in England when you told me you loved me,' he said quietly. 'You were open then, without your guard up. Nothing to lose, I suppose. It was the cards laid bare and I failed you. I failed you completely.'

Her heart was pounding against her ribcage so hard it was actually hurting, but she still managed to say, 'That's…that's gone, in the past. I…I'll be all right.'

'I love you, Sephy.'

She knew she couldn't have heard right.

'I love you so much it's a physical ache, all the time, no matter what I do. I've loved you from the first day you worked for me, or the first evening, to be precise, and I've fought it just as long. You were so brave that day, telling me how you felt and to hell with the consequences, and I smacked it all back in your face. Like I did when you said you loved me.'

The raw pain in his voice was real, the look in his face was real, but she couldn't believe what he was saying.

'You…you said—' She couldn't go on, and now he reached out and tenderly cupped her face in his strong hands.

'I know what I said. The big fellow—doesn't need anyone and doesn't care about anything. But I do need you and I care about you. You have to believe me.'

'No.' She couldn't. She *couldn't* dare to trust he meant it. 'You haven't been here, not in four weeks,' she said brokenly.

'And it's torn me apart to keep away.' He stroked his hand over the silky smooth skin of her cheek and she had to force herself not to turn her face into the caress. 'Why do you think I called you every night? I was desperate to hear your voice, to have something of you, but you were so ill in England, so fragile, and I owed you the chance to think clearly. If I'd asked you to marry me then you'd have always wondered if I meant it or if you were manoeuvred.'

What was he talking about, manoeuvred? she asked herself silently. If she thought he really meant this she would have swum back to England to see him.

'I had to give you the chance to get well and then decide, when your mind was clear and you were physically strong,' he said quietly. 'I owed you that if nothing else.'

Had he said *marry* him a few words back, or was she taking a trip on Maisie's planet Zargos again?

She strove for calm and said, tremblingly, 'You told me you don't believe in love and marriage and happy families. You said you couldn't change.'

'I also said that when you came to me it would be knowing exactly what you were doing and because you'd decided it was what you wanted,' he said softly, 'and I think the phrase is "hoisted with my own petard". I want you, Sephy, I want you so much physically it's driven me half mad. But then you know that.'

Did she? She hadn't known she had!

'I want the whole caboodle, Sephy—children and dogs and cats and whatever. I came here today to tell you that I love you, that I've loved and wanted you always. The thought of this other guy, this David, and not knowing where he'd fitted in your life was making me want to do murder. That's why I had to ask you that day, to find out what had happened and if you still loved him.'

'Love him? I didn't even know him,' she said shakily. She could feel the tears trickling down her face, and she hated that she was crying but she couldn't do a thing about it.

'Can you forgive me?' He bent and kissed the tears on her cheeks and she shuddered violently. 'Have I ruined everything? I know you love me, I saw it in your eyes when you turned round and saw me, but can you forgive me for what I've done to you?'

She was trembling so much he drew her close against the hard wall of his chest, and as she felt the accelerated beat of his heart she murmured helplessly, 'I'm frightened.'

'So am I.' He understood instantly and his voice was soft on the sun-warmed silk of her hair. 'There are parts of this love thing that aren't all they're cracked up to be; putting the whole of your life in someone else's hands, giving them the power to make or destroy you, thinking what it would be like if you had to live in a world without them—'

'Don't.' She moved back enough to gaze up into his face. 'Don't say that.'

It was an answer in itself, but still he said, 'Will you marry me, Sephy? Will you be my wife and let me love you and adore you and worship you all my life? Will you bear my children and be with me when their children are born? Will you sleep with me every night and wake with me every morning? Will you be my breath, my reason for living, the beat of my heart?'

'Oh, my love.' It was what she had always wanted to say but never had the right to express, and now she fell against him as he rained kisses on her face and throat in an agony of love and need. They clung together as though their bodies were already merging.

'I love you. You've got no idea how much I love you,' he murmured at long last, when she was flushed and bright-eyed, her lips swollen and her body straining into his. And then he reached in his pocket and brought out a little red velvet box, opening it to reveal an exquisite diamond engagement ring. 'For ever, Sephy.'

They were married in Sephy's hometown, in the little parish church in the village, and it seemed as though the world and his wife had turned out to see the local girl who had snared one of the biggest catches in the country.

The day was bright, and unseasonably warm for early October, and Sephy looked radiantly lovely in a long ivory gown trimmed with tiny gold daisies, her headdress and bouquet made up of fragile white baby's breath and a profusion of tiny gold daisies and fragile little gold and ivory orchids.

Maisie, as Sephy's bridesmaid, looked amazingly solemn and sedate for once, in her long gold dress and carrying a smaller version of Sephy's bouquet. She had even dyed her hair all one colour: a rather alarming shade of red, which should have clashed horribly with the dress but—Maisie being Maisie—actually looked rather good. But then with Sephy's mother giving the bride away and little Madge Watkins as Conrad's best man the wedding was never going to be a traditional one anyway. Just one filled with lots of love.

The winding path from the church door was thronged with well-wishers who hadn't been able to fit into the small thirteenth-century church as Sephy and Conrad emerged to the peal of church bells.

They stood for a moment, Conrad gazing down at his bride as Sephy looked adoringly up at her handsome groom, and no one seeing them could have doubted that this marriage was anything but a love match. 'Have I told you in the last minute that I love you, Mrs Quentin?' Conrad whispered in her ear as they began to walk down the confetti-strewn path.

'Yes, but don't let that stop you,' Sephy whispered back as the ribbon of smiling faces on either side of the path called out congratulations and good wishes. They had just reached the gnarled wooden gate at the end of the path when a red-faced, somewhat bloated man stepped straight out in front of them for a moment.

'Remember me, Sephy?'

It was said with confidence, but as Sephy glanced up for a moment it was clear she had no idea who he was, and then Conrad had whisked her away to the gleaming white Rolls-Royce he had hired to take them to the most exclusive hotel in the district where he had arranged a reception for family and friends and half the village.

David Bainbridge's eyes followed the car as it left the village green and his eyes, already bloodshot with the alcohol he'd consumed in large quantities daily since his father had lost all the family wealth on the Stock Exchange, were puzzled. That wasn't the girl he remembered; this one was a beauty. And she'd ignored him! Damn it, she hadn't even recognised him. And everyone had seen it.

But Sephy wasn't thinking about David Bainbridge, or anyone else but Conrad, as the rest of the day unfolded hour by entrancing hour. After a wonderful meal they danced the evening away, and Conrad was mean enough not to share her with anyone. Which suited the new Mrs Quentin just fine.

And then the evening drew to a close, all the guests were gone, and it was just the two of them alone in the magnificent bridal suite the hotel boasted.

They undressed each other slowly, and Sephy was surprised to find she felt no shyness as she stood naked before him. Perhaps the wonder and love in his eyes had something to do with it.

His passion was restrained at first, sensuous and coaxing as he held her close to him and stroked and petted her, his lips covering her face in tiny burning kisses before moving to her throat and then her breasts, teasing their peaks into taut hardness with his mouth and tongue.

When he finally lifted her into his arms and carried her over to the huge four-poster bed she was trembling and moist, her hands roaming over the hard-muscled wall of his chest as he leant above her for a moment, his blue eyes open and loving as he allowed her to look into his soul. 'I love you, my sweet wife,' he whispered softly. 'More than you could ever know.'

'Oh, Conrad...' She gripped his shoulders, pulling him down on her as she took his mouth with touchingly inexpert hunger.

'Shush, my darling, slowly, slowly,' he murmured with a faint touch of laughter in his voice. 'This has to be right for you.'

And then he took her into a time of pure enchantment, his lips warm as they kissed every inch of her body and his tongue entering all the secret places until she was crying out with abandoned pleasure, her body surging against his hands and mouth as she arched and pleaded for the release only he could give.

But still his control held, even though his body was betraying the fact that his desire was white-hot, as he continued to bring her to the very brink of fulfilment time and time again, only to draw back at the crucial moment and then begin the passionate ritual again.

When he finally possessed her he had brought her to fever-pitch, and the feel of him inside her, the knowledge that she was joined body and body to the man she loved with all her heart, made the exquisite physical pleasure unbearable.

As she felt his body convulsing with hers in perfect unity Sephy found herself transported to the outer spaces of time, a place where there was no tomorrow and no past, just a consuming present that utterly possessed her.

It was much later when she stirred in his arms, turning her head to open heavy-lidded eyes as she looked at him. And the devastating blue eyes were waiting for her, his voice slightly uneven as he said, 'Thank you, my darling. Thank you for giving yourself to me so completely.'

'I never guessed it was so...' She could find no words to describe the ecstasy. 'Is it always like that?' she asked dazedly.

'Never before. Not for me,' he whispered against the silky skin of her cheek before taking her mouth in a kiss that was tender beyond description. 'But I promise you, my darling, it will be like that for both of us from this night on.'

And Conrad Quentin had never been a man to break a promise.

**Getting down
to business in
the boardroom...
and the bedroom!**

A secret romance, a forbidden affair,
a thrilling attraction...

What happens when two people work
together and simply can't help falling in
love—no matter how hard they try to resist?

Find out in our new series of stories set
against working backgrounds.

Look out for

THE MISTRESS CONTRACT
by Helen Brooks, Harlequin Presents® #2153
Available January 2001

and don't miss

SEDUCED BY THE BOSS
by Sharon Kendrick, Harlequin Presents® #2173
Available April 2001

Available wherever Harlequin books are sold.

If you enjoyed what you just read,
then we've got an offer you can't resist!

Take 2 bestselling love stories FREE!

Plus get a FREE surprise gift!

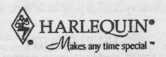

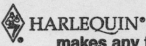